I0595698

John Young

The Province of Reason

A Criticism of the Bampton Lecture

John Young

The Province of Reason
A Criticism of the Bampton Lecture

ISBN/EAN: 9783337264109

Printed in Europe, USA, Canada, Australia, Japan

Cover: Foto ©Andreas Hilbeck / pixelio.de

More available books at **www.hansebooks.com**

UNIFORM WITH THIS VOLUME.

THE CHRIST OF HISTORY:

AN ARGUMENT GROUNDED ON THE FACTS OF HIS LIFE ON EARTH.

By JOHN YOUNG LL.D

Price 75 cents.

"It is an argument in favor of the Divinity of Christ, founded on the facts of his earthly life. It takes the lowest ground with the skeptic—excluding all miracles, and simply claiming the authenticity of those recorded facts which are free from question and all appearance of exaggeration or delusion. From these admitted facts, he constructs an argument to prove that Christ could not have been merely human, but must have been divine. What we admire in the argument is the candor and fairness with which it is conducted. The evangelic narratives are subjected to a rigid induction; nothing is relied on that is not unquestionable, and no conclusion drawn but such as is irresistible to every honest, logical mind. We have never seen this branch of Christian evidence so luminously and fairly treated. The writer is a severe and accurate thinker, and is evidently intent, throughout his whole argument, only upon obtaining the truth. For skeptical minds it must prove a most powerful and impressive work; while to all minds it will bring the great features of the Redeemer's life and character with so much freshness and force, that a deep impression can hardly be escaped. We regard it as an extraordinarily able and profitable volume."—*Evangelist.*

ROBERT CARTER & BROTHERS,

NEW YORK.

THE

PROVINCE OF REASON:

A CRITICISM OF

THE BAMPTON LECTURE

ON

"THE LIMITS OF RELIGIOUS THOUGHT."

BY

JOHN YOUNG, LL.D., EDIN.,

AUTHOR OF "THE CHRIST OF HISTORY," ETC.

NEW YORK:

ROBERT CARTER & BROTHERS,

No. 530 BROADWAY.

1860.

TO

The Right Hon. William Ewart Gladstone,

M. P. FOR THE UNIVERSITY OF OXFORD, AND FIRST VICE-CHANCELLOR OF
THE UNIVERSITY OF EDINBURGH,

THIS VOLUME,

WHICH ATTEMPTS TO EXAMINE THE PHILOSOPHIES

OF OXFORD AND EDINBURGH,

AND TO TEST THEIR LEGITIMATE RESULTS,

IS RESPECTFULLY DEDICATED,

BY HIS OBEDIENT HUMBLE SERVANT.

JOHN YOUNG.

London, 4th April, 1860.

PREFACE.

THERE are some things so true and so great, as to be independent of the obscurity or the fame of those who assert or deny them. The humblest individual, grasping them with his poor hand, possesses an advantage in their un-aided grandeur and force, which no superior abilities, acquirements, and culture can command.

To me, if the principles of the Bampton Lecture on the *Limits of Religious Thought* be conceded, the chief attribute of humanity, as constituted by the Great Father, is laid in the dust, the sacred Scriptures are an elaborate and meaningless pretence, the possibility of worship and of trust in the Supreme is destroyed, and, above all, the authority of conscience, and the immutable foundations of morality are undermined. These, I think, are reasons sufficiently powerful for attempting, even with inadequate means, to counteract the influence of a work which has found a much wider acceptance than metaphysical writings, generally, meet with in this country.

An independent, exhaustive, and formal discussion is not to be looked for here, of the great subject which is placed as the title of this volume. But I am altogether at fault, if by the criticisms and arguments which follow, the rightful Province of Reason be not made out, with some distinctness.

CONTENTS.

PAGE

SECTION SECOND.

CONCERNING APPLICATIONS OF LOGIC.

CHAPTER I.

PRELIMINARY CRITICISMS.

CHAPTER II.

"THE INFINITE," "THE ABSOLUTE," ETC.

CHAPTER III.

CAUSATION, ETC.

CHAPTER IV.

INCONCEIVABILITY OF "THE INFINITE."

CHAPTER V.

MISCELLANEOUS REASONINGS.

SECTION THIRD.

CONCERNING A PHILOSOPHY OF "THE UN-
CONDITIONED " ETC.

CHAPTER I.

RELATION OF THE SCOTTISH AND OXONIAN PHILOSOPHIES.

CHAPTER II.

MEANING OF "THE UNCONDITIONED," ETC.

SECTION FOURTH.

CONCERNING WRITTEN REVELATION.

CHAPTER I.

NECESSARY CONDITIONS.

CHAPTER II.

EVIDENCES OF REVELATION.

CHAPTER III.

REVELATION AND GOD.

SECTION FIFTH.

CONCERNING MORALITY AND MORAL SENSE.

CHAPTER I.

THE RELATIVE AND THE REAL.

CHAPTER II.

MODIFICATIONS OF MORALITY

CHAPTER III.

IMMUTABLE RIGHT AND WRONG.

SECTION SIXTH.

CONCERNING REASON AND FAITH.

SECTION FIRST.

INTRODUCTORY.

CHAPTER I.

REACTION.

Its inherent Vice—History of Speculaton—Oscillation from Extreme to Extreme—Impartial Investigation—Extreme Views of Bampton Lecture—Possible Medium.

THE old truism renews itself, with each age, in each struggle of opinions, bearing not partially on one side of a debated question, but honestly and equally on both. "Reaction rarely can be temperately wise or even simply just." The vice is inherent, ineradicable. The excess which provokes reaction, by a law as constant as any power in material nature, never fails to beget its counterpart, in a compensating excess, in the opposite direction. In the moment of keen, perhaps passionate debate, truth is never, *only and altogether*, with either of two antagonist sections, but partly with both, and often in marvellously equal proportion. A silent verity lies underneath every position, which has the force to attract around it resolute and honest adherents. There is, also, always lurking error in the selectest combination, let the party symbol embody ever so large an amount of truth. In the middle space between opposite extremes, verging now in the direction of the one, and again in the direction of the other, will be found that, which is far above all parties—the imperishable, the immutable, the divine.

The history of speculation reveals an incessant action and reaction of the mind of the ages, on the highest subjects of human thought. Instead of normal and progressive intellectual efforts, springing from within, from a wisely-balanced organism, obedient to its governing laws, men have been provoked or betrayed into opinions, have been hurried by prejudices, have been blindly enamored of some peculiar theory, perhaps their own, have been inflamed by a passion for victory, instead of a love for truth, and have acted in a spirit of partizanship and of rivalry; or they have obeyed the secret force of mental idiosyncracies, the existence of which in themselves they did not suspect. The result has been, successive oscillations, from extreme to extreme, always both right and both wrong, though in unequal degrees. The periods of dispassionate, catholic and steadily advancing investigation have been often remote from one another, rudely broken up by exaggerations and extravagances in one direction, which again have given birth to exaggerations

and extravagances, as great or greater in the opposite direction.

In this country, and at this moment, we seem
to be in the presence of a strong reaction, as well
in the department of mental philosophy, as in a
higher and more sacred sphere still. Opposite
schools are in collision ; no one, as yet, being acknowledged to have made good a permanent, exclusive occupation of the vantage ground. Such a
state of things may have its unquestionable bene-
fits, but there is also no small peril to the interests
of the highest truth, which may be sacrificed to
unfounded prejudices, or to the violence of unworthy passions. Perhaps only one thing is quite
certain, neither extreme of the opposing sections
will be wholly right, neither will be wholly wrong.
To discover that, in each, which is true, is the brave
and great work imposed on us by our age, and it
demands an impartial, searching, fearless, candid,
broad spirit of investigation.

No injustice is done to the celebrated work of
which we are about to venture a criticism, in saying
that it is the birth of a reaction, and is formally
designed to crush what is deemed an excessive and
dangerous rationalism. The lecturer states as much
in plain terms, and perhaps his deservedly admired
production bears upon it, sufficiently strongly
marked, the peculiar taint of a reactionary effort.
It is extreme—and here, without reasoning at all,

I may be allowed to cluster together in as few sentences as possible the first strong impressions produced on my own mind, which may also have been awakened in other minds, by this book. "It is extreme. It goes too far, to be quite within the law of equity and wisdom. It is too exterminating, too mercilessly destructive to be wholly merited. The effect also is utterly depressing and prostrating. Limited as human powers confessedly are, we shudder at abject intellectual denudation. It is one thing to admire heartily the extended and varied learning of an accomplished writer, the vigorous, sometimes eloquent periods that flow from his practised pen, his dialectic power, his logical subtilty, facility and courage, and to bow unfeignedly to the purity of his motives ; but it is quite another thing to consent to the justice of his conclusions. No. The impression abides and deepens—it is too much : it can not be true ; these principles are not in harmony with the deep convictions lodged in our nature, or with our most cherished hopes. Man must be able to know more of the Great Being than this writer will allow, *must* be able to reach some essentially true thoughts, respecting him. Nor is it doubtful, as he asserts it is, whether what constitutes virtue, moral excellence on earth among men, does also constitute virtue, moral excellence, among all orders of rational creatures. Conscience is not a temporary guide for this world only, is not the proclaimer of arbitrary distinctions and of mere human modifications of morality, but a divine voice in the soul, announcing what is eternally, immutably, universally right—right in itself, right for men, right for all rational beings, and right for ever and ever !

" Here is a high and extended argument—an elaborate book ! On what ? The Infinite, the Unconditioned, the Absolute. This author boldly goes into the region of inconceivable, *à priori* truths, the region of pure abstraction, the region of mere subjective logic. But the principle which he seeks to establish, is that the human mind is incapable of reasoning respecting the Infinite, incapable of conceiving the Infinite at all. Either his course is legitimate, and then his principle is demolished ; or his course is illegitimate and nugatory, and then his principle is yet undefended, unestablished. In any case, the false impression is created that human reason must be an irreconcilable foe to Christians and to Christianity, for nothing, it seems, will content them but to forbid imperatively every effort of reason to approach and adore the Great Being. And then, the evil is a grave and terrible one, that philosophy and religion alike are left surrounded with insoluble contradictions and impenetrable uncertainties. Is not the inference inevitable, that in this case, it is the part of wisdom to have as little as possible to do with either ?   So far as this book is concerned, many will fairly judge, that men have two and only two things before them.   Either, they must blindly accept as divine a revolution, whose external evidences—and with these the author maintains, and these only, reason has anything to do—it is literally impossible for myriads of them to examine, flattering themselves that this is faith ; or they must hopelessly surrender to a universal scepticism, calling this the light of reason."

Such, I believe, will be the first involuntary impressions of at least one class of minds, after·the perusal of these Lectures.   The question is, Can our first impressions bear second thoughts ?   Have they solid ground to rest upon ?   This remarkable book, professedly a defence of Revelation and a determination of the legitimate province of human reason, which has been welcomed cordially by a large portion of the public—dare we venture to suspect that it may, after all, be unsound in its fundamental principles, injurious to our most sacred interests, and dishonoring to one of the noblest endowments with which man has been gifted by his Maker.   Let us examine and judge.

CHAPTER II.

AMONG the minor, but decisive proofs of the
reactionary character, which pervades the work
before us, we mark the language, and especially
the tone in which rationalism so called, is described. The word, not without just occasion, has
come to be of bad odor; but in its etymological
sense, it is a faultless and excellent word. The
idea which it conveys is in entire harmony with
the nature of rational beings, is indeed *the* proper
and necessary demand of that nature.

Rationalism, rightly so called, is not a sectional,
but a universal faith. He who accepts cordially a
doctrine laid down in what he holds to be the
Book of Inspiration, does not hesitate to ask, and
expects to find, and *does* actually find, in most
cases, that, besides its external authoritative sanction, it is commended to his mind as true in itself,
and in harmony with other truths, and with those

general principles of belief, which belong to the constitution of our rational nature. Without exception, all who are capable of any mental effort, are conscious of a profound desire to discover a consistency between the dictates of their intelligence, and the articles of their faith, be that faith what it may. Very many things they may be unable perfectly to harmonize, and are satisfied to leave unsolved. But the effort in other directions is continued, notwithstanding. The desire is not extinguished. It is irrepressible. It belongs to our nature, to search and strive after inward harmony, after the reconciliation of things, which must be really one, whether we be able to discover their unity or not. So universal, so irrepressible, is this tendency, that it can only be looked upon as a law of our intelligence. And how vain to force back the rushing spirit of investigation, which obeys a power as mighty as that which governs the ocean in its ebb and flow! How vain to deter men from that to which the structure of their minds prompts them! How worse than vain, to stigmatize as crime an act of obedience to a constitutional principle!

The fact is, that the desire to reconcile our reason (using the word in its current popular sense, as synonymous with general human intelligence,) and our creed, be that creed what it may, Jewish, Christian, Mohammedan, or Pagan, rests on a

foundation as deep as any which our nature knows.
Let it be granted on the one hand that there is an
outward written revelation. But it is as surely
believed, on the other hand, that there is, also, an
inward unwritten revelation in our intelligent nature. Both have the same origin—they *must* be
perfectly harmonious. The voice of truth from
without must be essentially at one with the voice
of truth from within. *That* is the secret conviction of every mind, and it is indestructible. If
consciousness—as Sir William Hamilton, and we
presume Mr. Mansell, holds—be a revelation of the
facts of our inward being, it admits of no doubt
at all, that not the least authoritive portion of the
revelation must be that which embodies the data
of our higher reason. Our native cognitions, be
they many or few, the necessary truths lying in
the depths of our minds, our rational, and most of
all our moral intuitions, are to us the voice of the
Being who created us. And nothing can be more
certain than that He cannot contradict himself.
The outward, written revelation may contain treasures unknown to the inward revelation, and un-
utterably more precious. But so far as they go
the two *must be* in perfect, absolute harmony,
whether we be able to make it out, or not.

Even our lower reason—reason in the common
meaning of the word, the fair and sound conclusions
of the understanding proper, the comparing and

judging faculty—must be essentially at one with all truth. Imperfect and fallible as the human understanding is, it is the highest, it is *the* only instrument of judging, which our Maker has granted to us. Within its own sphere, wisely and rightly employed, it must be trustworthy ; at all events, we have nothing else, as rational beings, by which to compare, discriminate and affirm, or deny, in any case. But be the confidence which we repose in our mere understanding ever so limited, we are compelled to put unlimited trust in our higher reason, in the primitive data of our rational and moral nature. These must be altogether divine. The mysterious intuitions that result from no experience of ours, but come forth from that *locus principiorum*, to whose contents we have contributed nothing, and can never contribute anything, are a true and proper revelation from our Creator, and can only be in perfect harmony with every other communication from the same great source. We may mistake the inward message, as we may mistake the outward. There may be interpolations and various readings in the one, as there are also in the other. And different commentators and critics, American, Asiatic, African, European, German, French, British, according to their mental structure or their training, or their taste, may be prompted and may find it possible, to bring out different meanings from the one, as they have also from the other.   But the essential harmony of the two is indubitable.

This is the foundation, *the deep ground* of that tendency, which is strictly universal, though often unavowed, perhaps, even, often unperceived.   And shall it be denounced as wicked ?   Is the desire an impious one, to perceive the essential harmony between the nature with which our Creator has endowed us and what claims to be His written revelation ?   Is the mental effort to search till we discover, and as far as it is possible for us to discover this harmony, of such a nature, that a philosopher must frown upon it and forbid it peremptorily ?   On the contrary, is it not in every way becoming, and right, and imperative, forced on us by a clamorous want within, and demanded, as a sacred duty, springing out of veneration of the Great Being ?

It is not denied that there are evils, possible and real evils, connected with the free exercise of the understanding within the domain of religion.   Instead of humility, and reverence, and faith, a hardened, presumptuous, impious spirit shall create most revolting confusion between the respective claims of man and his Creator.   But every good thing on this earth must be accepted, if accepted at all, with grievous deductions.   Liberty always and everywhere, is in danger of degenerating into licentiousness, yet with all its chances of abuse it may not be exchanged, one instant, for the Upas shade of despotism. Truth in like manner may be pushed to extreme, and may pass into extravagance and absurdity, but it must be left perfectly free nevertheless, exposed to all manner of perversions, and is only endangered by pretended safeguards, material or spiritual. And that desire, deeply based in our nature, the desire not to bring the dictates of our intelligence to revelation or revelation to them, for either would be dishonest, but to make out, ever in greater extent, the real and perfect harmony between the two ; this desire is not to be crushed, to whatever possible evils it may give rise. It cannot be crushed. Desire or do what we may, it *will* not be crushed ; and the attempt to crush it is ignoble as it is futile. Virtually, it is the old struggle revived, ever in vain, between might and right, between authority and intelligence, between blind superstition and enlightened faith. What the faggot and the fire of other times failed to accomplish is not likely to be accomplished by a ponderous and rigorous dialectic, a hard, cold, and passionless logic. Divine Revelation and right reason have one source ; it is a very sacred thing to strive to *see*, it would be very wrong not to strive to *see* that they utter one voice.

But Rationalism, so called, has a general evil reputation. Deservedly it has an evil reputation, owing to misapplications and abuses sanctioned by some of its nominal disciples, perhaps amongst us, certainly, in other quarters. The power of the understanding has been exaggerated and a much wider province has been claimed for the human faculties, than belongs to them rightfully. The most sacred authority has been invaded and the proper liberty of scientific criticism has passed, in some instances, to licentiousness. This is the extreme on one side, and it is worthy of just condemnation. But it is not just to represent, as the Bampton lecturer has done, the extreme as the thing itself—the extreme, too, in its very worst form, a form unknown to this country, limited, at all events, to a few solitary individuals who reject Chistianity altogether, and are, certainly, not worthy of prominent consideration, or entitled to the rank of leaders of public opinion.

CHAPTER III.

GERMANY is the imagined birth-place and home
of rationalism proper, which, as currently understood, simply means the wildest infidelity. The
philosophy and theology of that country are asso-
ciated in the minds of many with all that is law-
less, absurd, and impious. And certainly, in no
other region, shall we find any thing answering to
the modes of thought which are exposed in the
Bampton Lecture. Those who are unacquainted
with Germany can scarcely be capable of doing
justice, either to the errors which the lecturer
assails, or to his method of combatting them.
There was needed for most of his readers, I apprehend, in order to intelligent appreciation, some
account—if touching only the leading, uppermost

points—of the speculations of Kant, Fichte, Schelling, and Hegel, to whom chiefly allusion is made. I find myself obliged, for my own sake, and that my future statements and reasonings may be understood, to attempt something of this kind, though it can only be very imperfect and very general. The difficulty is unusually great, of putting into small compass, an account at all intelligible and satisfactory.

My statement can have little value save that, as the mode in which a common mind has striven to bring a hard subject within its conception, it may bě the more easily apprehensible by ordinary men.

Emanuel Kant is esteemed the arch-heretic of Germany, the father of a rationalism, which for more than half a century flooded the Continent, almost unchecked, and well-nigh swept away the most sacred mental heritage of the nation. Were this true, or anything like truth, that grave and good man must have thoroughly misunderstood his own office and actual work. His conscious and determined aim was directly the reverse. At a time when the idealism of Hume had found disciples all over Europe, and when the materialism and atheism of Voltaire, D'Holbach, and the Encyclopædists had infected Germany to its very core, and were spreading fast and far, Kant stood forward a philosophic, I might say, a religious reformer. He, *at least,* honestly *intended* to build up an impregnable defence for philosophy and for religion against the worst assaults of scepticism. If the actual effect was widely different from the original intention—if, as has been said with some bitterness, but also with a little truth, he has only laid a more thoroughly logical basis for infidelity— at least his sincerity is unquestionable. And his philosophy, now better understood and more fairly applied, forms a grand landmark in the progress of European enlightenment. Many who vehemently cry out against the transcendental nonsense of Kant, the same persons who eagerly take refuge in the system of Sir William Hamilton, as the bulwark of religion, are little aware of the actual relation which these two philosophical chiefs bear to one another.

There are several and very important points of difference between the Scottish and the Kantian philosophies. But, passing over the terminology, which, in the one case, is simple, and in the other, is barbarous and nearly unintelligible, none who are acquainted with both, and without prejudice against either, will dispute that the philosophy of Sir William Hamilton is virtually and essentially the philosophy of Kant. The points of resemblance are leading and striking. Consciousness, the authoritative witness of all mental phenomena, is the basis of both. The two mental forms of time and space, which mold the acts of consciousness, are common to both. So also are the fact of pure *à priori* truths made known by consciousness, and the two principles of universality and necessity by which such truths are tested. So also is the grand, general distribution of all the phenomena of consciousness into those of knowledge, and feeling, and conation, or desire and will. And on what may be called Sir William Hamilton's great principle, of a philosophy of *the conditioned* being alone possible, has anything more explicit been uttered than these words of Kant ? " This refusal of our reason to afford a satisfactory answer to speculative questions, *extending beyond this life*, is a hint from it, to divert our self-cognition from fruitless *transcendant speculation* to fruitful practical use ; which, although it is always directed only to objects of experience, still takes up its principle at a higher point, and thus determines its procedure, as if our destiny extended infinitely far beyond experience, and consequently out beyond this life."[*]

But notwithstanding the close relation of the two philosophies, it is not difficult to account for the aversion—to use no harsher term—with which Kant has been and is regarded among us, and for the actual, evil results to which his system gave occasion in his own country. That all our knowledge can be only relative, not absolute, that it is of phenomena only and not of things *in se*, is not

* *Kritik der reiner Vernunft, Seite* 421. Frankfort, 1791.

peculiar to him, but is equally maintained by Sir William Hamilton. The chief vulnerable points in the Kantian system, the sources of that fatal direction which it gave to speculation, appear to me to be the two following :

I. The false valuation of the subjective and the objective respectively. The *non-ego*, with Kant, is next to nothing ; the *ego* is all but everything. The reality of the *non-ego* is not denied. He finds it in consciousness. He finds it also a pure understanding-cognition, under the category of substance. But it is reduced to the smallest possible minimum. There *is* an unknown substratum of phenomena ; but the phenomena, excepting this inherence in an unknown substratum, are wholly dependent on the *ego*, a result arising from the laws of our sensibility and the forms of the understanding. The *non-ego* is all but phenomenal, far more subjective than objective. Even the *ego* itself is, in a wide sense, phenomenal ; that is to say, the *ego* of consciousness is only the manifested, the phenomenized *ego*. *The I*, thinking, feeling, or willing, is a phenomenon of consciousness. But there is something else, and far more, which never comes up as phenomenon. The real *ego* is behind, underneath—an unknown substratum, substance. It is impossible not to see the tendency of this to lead either to scepticism, on the one hand, or to pure subjective idealism, on the other—a tendency which was too speedily developed in both directions.

II. A more fatal portion still of the Kantian system is that, wherein what are held to be the necessary contradictions of the pure reason, are set forth. This is the portion, it must be noted, which in its spirit, and, to some extent, in its very form, has been reproduced in the Bampton Lecture ; to be followed, there is reason to fear, unless some sufficient corrective and repellant be forthcoming, by not less lamentable consequences. The doctrine of creation, that of identity and immortality, that of liberty and necessity, and that of the necessary existence of the Deity, are those wherein Kant concludes, there exists for the pure reason inevitable contradiction. The sphere to which these doctrines belong, according to Kant, is that of the unconditioned, and it is this sphere, from which it is the great purpose of the Bampton lecturer to show, there can arise nothing but contradiction to the human mind. Only in ignorance can it be imagined, that while Kant propounds antinomies in one region, the English philosopher discovers them in another. The sphere is the same to both, and, virtually, the work of both is the same. But there is *this* marked difference : Kant, applying a severe logic to the criticism of the pure reason, having discovered what he deemed natural and necessary contradictions, was obliged in stern honesty to expose them. But he labors, though unsuccessfully, to show how they arise, so as to save, as far as may be, the authority of reason. The English philosopher seems to go to his work with good will, and with the distinct aim, not to make the best of what may be confessedly bad, but to make the bad worse, and still worse, if possible. He seems to exhibit satisfaction, not sorrow, in humbling and maiming human reason, and fixing on it the charge of weakness and error. Be this as it may, at least Kant knew full well the inherent tendency of that portion of his system to which we have referred. " Reason," he says " is hereby led into the temptation, either of abandoning itself to a sceptical hopelessness, or of assuming a dogmatical pride, and carrying its head stiffly as to certain assertions, without granting a hearing or justice to the arguments for the contrary. Both ways are the death of a sound philosophy, although the first (scepticism) may be called the euthanasia of pure reason."*

Fichte was at first the disciple, and always the reverent and loving admirer, of the Königsberg sage. But his genius was too real and too kingly to be controlled. Unhappily imbibing the latent errors of the Kantian system, he developed with fatal success the special evil which inhered in them.

I. On the one hand, the exaggeration of the

* *Kritik*, s. 434.

subjective, carried so high by Kant, was carried still higher by Fichte. If the *ego* were really of such moment as the master had shown it was, it must be of yet greater moment still, the disciple argued. The *non-ego*, reduced to the smallest possible minimum by the one, was reduced to *nil* by the other. The *ego* and its manifestations included everything. Knowledge can only be of the acts of consciousness ; consciousness cannot transcend itself. What is within, it can bear witness to, what is without, if there be existence without, we can never know. Our inward sensations, thoughts, acts, and changes of whatever kind, belong to the sphere of our knowledge ; nothing else does. External phenomena are wholly the creation of the *ego*, wholly the result of subjective changes and laws. An external substratum or substans, even if such a thing existed, we have no possible means of reaching. We can know only what is within the *ego*, its modes and its acts. Still further, as Kant had shown that the *ego* of consciousness was only phenomenal, and that the real *ego* "*in se*" was unrevealed, Fichte extended the principle yet farther. With him the *ego* became not so much individual in this or that person, as absolute and universal in humanity. And how near this was to a pure, subjective pantheism, it is not hard to perceive.

May we here venture a humble, yet sincere word

on behalf of the man, one of the brightest and noblest sons of the German fatherland, without faltering in condemnation of the system ? Presently, I shall have occasion to produce the words of Schelling, when he vehemently resisted the charge of pantheism which was brought against him, with greater force of evidence, than against any of his philosophical comperes. But as vehemently and as sincerely did Fichte resent the same charge, and that of atheism also, of which he was accused. I do not profess to explain how it was ; I do not understand it. But it seems, as if the personal faith of none of the German philosophers could be righteously measured, by the sytems which they founded. These systems, without exception, starting from a mere assumption, were severely wrought out by them, on the principles of what they deemed the soundest logic, were held by them as sacred, hard-gotten possessions, and in the region of abstract thought, ruled over them with absolute sway. But it would seem that all the while their real, personal life, their moral convictions, and their religious faith, were quite apart, as if in a totally different sphere. In my humble judgment, the metaphysical speculations of Fichte, beginning with a mere *petitio principii*, are as baseless and as wild as they are calculated to be deeply injurious and dishonoring to the Great Being. But the religious and moral region of his soul, in some unaccountable way, must have been preserved notwithstanding. Scarcely anything loftier, purer, more touching, and more inspiring in moral sentiment, is to be found anywhere, than Fichte has indited. The lustre which encircles his memory, to my mind, is more spiritual, more genial, more human, than that which gathers around almost any other of the great names of Germany. His life was a noble one. His death approached the heroic ; and his character was one of rare elevation and purity. Enough of this. There was a second direction, in which the latent evil of the Kantian system was developed by Fichte.

II. The weakness and untrustworthiness of pure reason, as shown by Kant, created an intense recoil in the mind of one who, though a skilled logician, had more of sentiment, and soul, and daring genius in his constitution, than of the dialectic spirit. He rushed to the opposite extreme. The authority of reason *must* be paramount. He would accept no other guide. But this issue again was powerfully helped from another and very different quarter than the Kantian philosophy. The short, suffering, self-denying course of Benedict Spinoza had been extensively productive, too productive, for its effects were in a fearfully evil direction. Perhaps no single man, not excepting even Leibnitz himself, ever exerted so deep an influence on all the leading souls of Germany as did the persecuted Jew. Leibnitz may have touched the national mind at many more points, but his influence in the one direction in which Spinoza especially wrought, was nothing like so profound or enduring. It has seemed to me that the wild, reckless, almost insane spirit, so constantly flashing out both in the philosophy and the theology of Germany, is to be ascribed, in very great part, to the sway which the writings of Spinoza had secured. And Fichte's was a soul to be struck more than most by their unflinching boldness and their tremendous sweep. Having, besides, altogether renounced the reality of the objective, it became a necessity for him to maintain so much the more determinedly, the reality and validity of the subjective. If the conclusions of reason were hopelessly contradictory, as Kant's antinomies seemed to show, there was nothing for him evermore to trust to. But, in Spinoza, he found at once a high assertion and a noble testimony to the supremacy of reason. Here was a mighty effort of the subjective faculty, a system professedly founded on, and entirely wrought out by, pure reason. He took his own course, he did not accept the details, but he was hereby fortified and secured in the principle.

There is wonderful fascination in the system of Spinoza as a piece of mere abstraction, a pure creation of the intellect. It is simple, clear, apparently exhaustive and unanswerable. *Substans* and modes, subject and attributes, apparently *must* include all being. Can there be any higher generalization than this ? Except for the one omission of the idea of causality, fatal to the metaphysical, but still more to the moral side of the speculation, the answer must have been, No ; there *can* be no higher generalization. But this fundamental omission produces, on the one hand, a pure objective Pantheism ; and, on the other hand, a universal and terrific fatalism.

Did not the mind of Germany recoil at once, and for ever, from such a system ? Formally, it did ; that is to say, Spinoza found few professed disciples. But his influence was deep and far extended, notwithstanding. A tone was given to speculation, and a cast of thought was inspired and diffused, which live to this day. The intellectual vigor and daring of the man, his wonderful logical faculty, his lofty generalization, and his profound power of abstraction, were captivating. But, above all, his memory was loved, for his sufferings, his moral integrity and intrepidity, and, if the testimony of Schleiermacher is to be accepted, for his piety. Unaccountably, the Berlin theologian deliberately honors him as " the holy, though rejected Spinoza." And many of the philosophers and theologians of Germany shared, perhaps to this day share, his enthusiasm. These are the words in which Schleiermacher exalts him : " the high world-spirit penetrated him, the illimitable was his beginning and his end, the universe his only and eternal love. In holy innocence and deep humility, he saw himself mirrored in the eternal world : and perceived, at the same time, how he, likewise, was the world's mirror. Full of religion was he, and full of the Holy Ghost ; and, therefore, stands he alone and unapproachable, a master in his art, but lifted high above profane association, without disciples, and without citizenship."*

The influence of Spinoza on the tone, if not the substance of Fichte's speculations, is most manifest. On those of Hegel, we shall find it is yet more manifest still. But it is most of all palpable and pervading in the philosophy of Schelling. *That* is virtually and truly, though not formally, Spinozism, another name for Pantheism ; and hence, the charge was broadly preferred against Schelling, and with the very strongest apparent ground. How indignantly and utterly he cast it from him, these words of his will show : " God is that which is in itself, and only from itself can be conceived ; but the finite is necessarily in another, and only from this can be conceived. Clearly, in consequence of this distinction, things are separated from God ; not merely, as might appear from the doctrine of modifications superficially considered, in degree and

* *Werke*, 1st Band, s. 100. Berlin, 1843.

through their limitations, but *toto genere*. Whatever their relation to God may be, they are absolutely divided from Him by this, that they can exist only in and through another (namely Him), so that the conception of them is a dependent one, which, without the conception of God, would be in no way possible. He, on the contrary, is alone the self-sufficient, original, self-affirming Existence, and everything else can be essentially related to Him, only as affirmed by Him, and dependent on Him. Only on this hypothesis are the attributes of things (their eternity, for example) valid. God is eternal in his own nature ; things are eternal only dependently on Him, and as consequences of his existence. Just owing to this difference, all individual things taken together cannot, as is often asserted, constitute God. By no kind of combination can that, which in its own nature is derived, pass into that which in its own nature is underived."*

Can words be more clear, more exact, more strong, than these ? The man who uttered them, surely, could be no real pantheist in his soul ; but he certainly was in his philosophical system. It is a striking instance of what I have ventured to suppose, though I am altogether unable to explain it, the entire separation, as if into two totally different and widely apart regions—the entire separation, in

* *Schriften*, 1st Band, s. 404. Landschut, 1809.

the German metaphysicians, of the speculative intellect from the moral convictions and life.   .

The absolute *assumed* by Schelling—(always the outset is pure assumption)—is virtually the universal *substans* of Spinoza, and the *ego* and *non-ego* of Schelling are virtually the two modes of Substance, thought and extension, as evolved by Spinoza. But, further, Schelling seeks to show that the *ego* and *non-ego*, though separate, are also one ; that subject and object, though apart, are also identical. There are two poles of Being, like the negative and positive extremes of the magnet, the center being the indifference-point, in which the two meet and are one. The Absolute is an infinite subject-object, evolving itself in two forms, as mind and as matter. There is a process of evolution, from the Absolute, into intelligence on the one hand, and into external nature on the other hand. There is also a process of resumption in which mind and matter are restored to identity in the Absolute, are absorbed in the essential unity of the Great Whole.

It is curious and startling to find, that the knowledge, by us, of the Absolute is also reached through a process of absorption and identification. The organ of this highest knowledge, which is possessed only by a gifted few of the human race, Schelling calls intellectual intuition. The soul in its upward stretch towards the Absolute, rises beyond the sphere of consciousness, passes away as out of itself, loses itself for the time, in identity with pure Being, in absorption into pure Being. Thus identified and absorbed, and only thus, it comes to know the Absolute.

From what absurdity and what contradictions this intellectual-intuition theory is obviously inseparable, need not here be shown. But it is impossible not to connect it at once with Jacob Boehme, with Tauler, with Eckart, and with the whole mystic school from the earliest period. Schelling is no more the metaphysician, but the undisguised mystic, whatever that may involve. There was needed a mind far more philosophic and more systematic than his, if anything enduring were to come out from the materials which he had alienated from their true sphere.

Hegel is pre-eminently the philosopher of Germany—always excepting Kant, who in his originality, in the depth and sweep of his views, and in his logical facility and power, is unsurpassed. Hegel had less of poetry and of spiritual insight than Schelling, and far less of genius and of soul than Fichte, but he had more of the legislative and methodizing faculty than either, had more entire mastery of logic, was more inured to extended abstraction, and altogether was gifted with a more subtle, more comprehensive and more indomitable intellect.

The Absolute is the starting-point of the Hegelian philosophy. In the farthest, utmost regress of thought, we reach *the Absolute*, a bare idea, a pure abstraction, the purest and most abstract of all abstractions, a something infinite, unconditioned —for with Hegel, the Absolute, the Infinite, the Unconditioned are the same and applied to one idea—the *ultima thule* of thought, the last, dim, naked point in the backward stretch of the reason. Beyond this we cannot pass, but this we reach, and with this, therefore, philosophy must begin "das absolute," the boundless, aloof from all limitation, relation, condition or dependence, nothing substantial, actual, as we speak, far less material, I had almost said physical, but only pure, mere idea, which to him was alone entity." The Absolute" was the unbeginning, eternal Idea, and phenomena were the decomposition and reconstruction, the egress and regress of the Idea. The analysis of the Absolute, therefore, would be a true re-thinking of the stupendous, aboriginal, abysmal thought ; it would be the key of the universe, for the universe is only the evolution of the Idea. The higher we can ascend in the analytic movement, the nearer we must come to *very* reality. Hence the process of thought, as thought, of all thought, must reveal the true unfolding of the " Absolute Idea." A thought as such, is never a unity. Something is distinguished from some other thing, and the two combined and unified form the thought.

What then are the elements into which the Absolute Idea may be resolved ? What is the result of this last and highest analysis ? I. Das Absolute ist das Seyn. The boundless, the unconditioned, the absolute is, first of all, *Being.* It is—but that is all—it is mere, bare Being. "Es ist dies, die (im Gedanken) schlechthin anfängliche, abstracteste, und dürftigste,"*—"the barest, nakedest, most impoverished idea, possible to be formed"—mere Being, mere existing, wide, boundless, undistinguished, undetermined by anything, in any way—no attributes, no consciousness. II. Das Absolute ist das Nichts—is nothing, non-being. "Das reine Seyn," says Hegel, "ist nun die reine Abstraction, damit das absolut-negative, welches, gleichfalls unmittelbar genommen, das Nichts ist. Es folgte hieraus, die zweite Definition des Absoluten, dasz es das Nichts ist."† "Pure being is pure abstraction, and consequently the absolute-negative, which in like manner, directly taken, is nothing. There follows from this the second definition of the Absolute, that it 'is nothing,'—non-being." I must yet again employ Hegel's own words—"Nur in-und um-dieser Unbestimmtheit-willen, ist es Nichts ; ein unsagbares, sein Unter-

---

* *Encyclopädie Die Lehre vom Seyn,* s. 99. Heidelberg 1827.
† Seite 100.

sobied von dem Nichts ist eine blosse Meinung."
—"Only through and on account of this undefin-
edness (unconditionedness) is Being=non-being—
a thing incapable of being expressed, its difference
from non-being is a bare notion." Being, in the
sense intended by Hegel, mere being, without attributes and without consciousness, is absolutely
unconditioned, has nothing to mark it, to define
it, to make it a thing. And non-being, in like
manner, is absolutely unconditioned, has nothing,
and can have nothing, to mark or define it ; for it
is nothing. Here, therefore, in this respect, das
Seyn ist das Nichts, Being is non-Being.

Being and non-being are the same, amount to
the same. Both are alike absolutely unconditioned, and both, on the same ground, are alike
included, and nothing else is included, in the Absolute. These, then, are the two elements, which
enter alike into the Absolute Idea, and are con-
tradistinguished. In the seeming unity of every
idea, there needs a " widerspruch," some one thing
to be set against another, a positive and a negative ; and only through their union is the formation of a distinct idea possible. *Das Seyn*, mere
unconscious being, would for ever have remained
unconscious=non-being. There was needed, *ein
Anders-seyn*—other being. Only by meeting something else, could *das Seyn*, distinguish itself, become conscious of itself. But the original, *Anders-*

seyn, must be " das Nichts,"—non-being ; nothing else was possible according to the conception. And hence *this,* namely, non-being, was the medium through which, alone, self-distinction and self-consciousness were reached by the *Seyn.* So that the formula was logically true. " Das Nichts ist **das** Seyn,"—non-being *is* being; it became *as* being to the *Seyn,* it was the *Anders-seyn*—other being, **an** actual thing. Alone, they were each as nothing, but together they *grow* to something ; they result in " das werden,"—the becoming : there is an evolution from them into consciousness ; there is the formation of a distinct idea, a passing into reality. Thus we have the Absolute Idea resolved into its elements, " das Seyn, das Nichts (das Andersseyn), das Werden." This is the Eternal, Unbeginning process. The universe is no other than this evolution of " The Idea," an everlasting becoming, a ceaseless growing up into reality, that is, *ideal* reality ; for with Hegel there is no other. Ideas are things, and there **are** no real things, but ideas !

Only a mere fragment of the Hegelian *Schema,* have I attempted to open. Let it suffice. The fatal, mortal vice is palpable as sunlight. The basis of the speculation is pure, mere assumption. There never was, never could be, such an absolute as is supposed, or such an evolution of unconscious into conscious being, save in the brain of the dreamer. But we are compelled to admire the man, however we judge of the system. His prodigious subtlety, and his giant grasp of the severest abstractions create unmixed amazement. And many grand, pure, noble thoughts has he left behind, which must live, and kindle life, wherever they are received. But it is almost past belief, that a sane and honest mind should have surrendered itself to such utter and perfect wildness of speculation as we have exposed ; and still more past belief that multitudes of sane and honest men should have caught the infection, and with almost the enthusiasm of piety, have carried the madness of logic to a more outrageous height still. But it is true.

No complaint could be made against the Bampton lecturer, for any strong and severe language he may have used, had it applied only to the wild extremes of German speculation ; especially since, in Hegel's own *Philosophy of Religion*, and in the writings of Feuerbach, Bauer, Strauss, and many besides, it has been shown to what ruinous lengths it may be carried, when brought to bear on the most sacred of all subjects. But the lecturer, throughout his celebrated volume, and, as it appears to me, without guard or reserve, has identified this country, its philosophers and theologians, not only with German speculation, but with its very extreme and worst forms. The following quotations, a few out of many, I may be allowed to put forward in evidence of this :

"The rationalist . . . assigns to some superior tribunal the right of determining what (in revelation) is essential to religion and what is not; he claims the privilege of accepting or rejecting any given revelation, wholly or in part, according as it does or does not satisfy the conditions of some higher-criterion, to be supplied by the human consciousness." (pp. 4, 5.) Rationalism proceeds— "by paring down supposed excrescences. Commencing with a preconceived theory of the purpose of a revelation, and of the form which it ought to assume, it proceeds to remove or reduce all that will not harmonize with this leading idea." (p. 6.) "Rationalism tends to destroy revealed religion altogether, by obliterating the whole distinction between the human and the divine. If it retain any portion of revealed truth, as such, it does so, not in consequence, but in defiance, of its fundamental principle." (p. 16.) "The fundamental position of rationalism is, that man by his own reason can attain to a right conception of God." (p. 37.) In a way certainly not characterized by dignity, rationalists are thus addressed : "Fools, to dream that man can escape from himself, that human reason can draw aught but a human portrait of God ! They do but substitute a marred and mutilated humanity for one exalted and entire, they add nothing to their conception of God as he is, but only take away a part of their conception of man ; . . . and what is the *caput mortuum* which remains, but only the sterner features of humanity, exhibited in repulsive nakedness." (p. 18.) "Our rational philosopher strips off from humanity just so much as suits his purpose, and ' the residue thereof he maketh a god,'—less pious in his idolatry than the carver of the graven image, in that he does not fall down unto it and pray unto it, but is content to stand afar off and reason concerning it." (p. 19.)   "Surely downright idolatry is better than this rational worship of a fragment of humanity. . . . Unmixed idolatry is more religious than this. . . . Undisguised atheism is more logical." (p. 20.)

As descriptive of rationalism, Mr. Mansell produces the following quotations from the darkest portions of Hegel's logic, nearly unintelligible, one may surmise, to English readers :—"The logical conception is the absolute divine conception itself, and the logical process is the immediate exhibition of God's self-determination to Being." (p. 30.) "Religion is the divine spirit's knowledge of himself, through the mediation of the finite spirit." (p. 31.) "The kingdom of philosophy is truth, absolute and unveiled. It contains in itself the exhibition of God as he is in his eternal essence, before the creation of a finite world." (p. 31.)

In connection with these, are quotations less dark, but not less revolting, from Strauss, from Fichte, from Schelling, from Feuerbach, from Marheincke, and from August Comte. After a reference to the philosophical Christ of Hegel and the mythical Christ of Strauss, the lecturer cries out with passionate indignation : "These be thy gods, O philosophy ! these be the metaphysics of salvation !" (p. 161.)

I venture to think that one and all of these passages, and especially the whole taken together, are not called for either in spirit or in direct expression. I venture to think that they are not true and not just, that scarcely a single one of them is true or just, as applied to any philosophical or theological school in this country, or even almost to any solitary individuals. As for Fichte, Schelling, Feuerbach, and Strauss, they belong very much to the past, even in Germany. It cannot be denied that the spirit which they, and especially the first and brightest of them, Fichte, awoke and diffused, still breathes in many a page of modern German literature. But it deserves remark that no one of them has founded a school called after his name, or can number of actual disciples beyond a few scattered units. Strauss has formally receded from his earlier course, without abjuring it, and has entered on the field of sober historical science, far away from the mythic region. Hegel alone can be said to survive as the founder of a system, and he is the parent of several separate schools.   In the thirty years that have passed since his death, they have arisen, each differing, on some points, from the master, but all standing by his method and deeply imbued with the spirit of his philosophy.   But where in this country shall we look for the faintest image of the Hegelian rationalism ?   It does not exist.   Since the days of Locke, if we except the school of English Platonists, and the irregular and incomplete efforts of Mr. Coleridge, it must be confessed with sorrow, that the philosophy of England has been only descendental.   Our transcendentalism is the merest *nominis umbra.*   We have, it is true, as we always have had, and certainly not in greater number or of more formidable character, now than in other times, individual writers, avowedly opposed to divine revelation on various grounds.   It is true, also, that translations of Strauss' *Life of Jesus* are circulated to some noticable extent, and that the atheism of Comte has been epitomised and put into an English dress.   Nor is it denied, that here and there may be found stray sentiments and an occasional cast and method of thought which can be distinctly traced to a Hegelian source.   But among our philosophical writers, and especially among our theologians, of whatever class, in this country—and it is theologians especially that are formally addressed in the Bampton Lecture—where is there anything answering, or even in the most distant way approaching to that rationalism which, in such dark lines, is marked off in the passages which have been quoted?   There is not any such thing.

It is scarcely just or worthy of philosophy or of religion, to exhibit a picture which finds its counterpart only in the growth of a foreign country, as if it truly represented some rationalistic school in this country.   By all means, if there be individuals, clerical or lay, who have seemed to attach higher authority to human reason than is meet, and to treat great and sacred questions in too free and rash a spirit, let their sentiments be met on their own proper ground and exposed and corrected. But it is a very different procedure—one essentially faulty—to identify a number of persons not formerly indicted, but perfectly well known, with a system which, as a whole, they would utterly repudiate, to identify them with the very worst details of that system.   The effect of this—I do not believe the conscious design, but the actual effect of this—must be to create against earnest and able and upright men a prejudice, of which they are wholly undeserving.

There *is* a rationalism—it must be held all the more firmly, because the too indiscriminate and too strong language of the Bampton Lecture would blind us to the fact ; there *is* a rationalism, not German—if so invidious and offensive a use of an honored national name may be pardoned—not German and not infidel, and not presumptuous, and not godless—a rationalism reverent, humble, pious, which, unless we be false to the constitution of our minds, false to what is higher than our minds, eternal truth, and false to the Great Being, the Father of our minds and the Fountain of truth, we dare not, must not, never must forego.

SECTION SECOND.

CONCERNING APPLICATIONS OF LOGIC.

CHAPTER I.

PRELIMINARY CRITICISMS.

Method of Bampton Lecture—Laid down, Abandoned—Over-
confidence—Difficulties of Investigation—Virtually, Hamilton's
Arguments — "Infinite" distinguished from "Absolute"—
Groundless—Essentially same.

THE method of discussion, proposed in the
Bampton Lecture, has all the advantage of being
faultlessly logical. It is perfectly fair to say, as
the writer does, that "the primary and proper
object of criticism is not religion, natural or revealed, but the human mind in its relation to religion." (p. 24.) It is added, "rightly or wrongly,
men will think of these things (the truths of religion), and a knowledge of the laws under which
they think, is the only security for their thinking
soundly." (p. 32.) "A philosophy of religion," he
says with great distinctness, "may be attempted
from two opposite points of view—either as a philosophy of the object of religion, that is to say, as
a scientific exposition of the nature of God, or as
a philosophy of the subject of religion, that is to
say, as a scientific inquiry into the constitution of
the human mind, so far as it receives and deals

with religious ideas". (p. 34.) Of the second method, which the lecturer is to adopt, it is said, "its primary concern is with the operations and laws of the human mind, and its special purpose is to ascertain the nature, the origin, and the limits of the religious element in man." (p. 35.) Before dealing with the object of religion, God, "we need a preliminary examination of the conditions of human thought." (p. 37.) In this way, we reach "the limits of our own powers and the consequent distinction between what we may and what we may not seek to comprehend." (p. 36.) "We must begin with that which is within us, not with that which is above us, with the philosophy of man, not with that of God." (p. 65.)

Such is the order of discussion. But, curiously enough, it is not sooner announced than abandoned. Instead of commencing with an examination of the human mind, in order to ascertain the conditions and limits of human thought, the lecturer turns aside to expose the contradictions and confusions of German rationalism. For the time, he follows a method exactly the opposite of that on which he had determined, *the* method which begins not with the subject of theology, man, but with the object of theology, God. The temptation must have been powerful, which thus hurried him in the face of the order which he himself had imposed on the discussion, that he might reduce to absurdity the attempts of German rationalists, to philosophize respecting the Infinite. "We can not," says he, "legitimately approach the object of theology, God, until a previous inquiry has determined for us the limits of our powers of thought, and what we may, and what we may not seek to comprehend." But straightway, we are led down to the deepest of the reasonings, about the most incomprehensible aspects of that which the lecturer pronounces to be all incomprehensible together. Without attaching immoderate importance to this violation of order, it is nevertheless very significant in a professed and disciplined logician.

The opening sentence, with which the lecturer introduces the strictly argumentative part of his work, deserves a little notice from us here. "There are three terms, *familiar as household words* in the vocabulary of philosophy, which must be taken into account in every system of metaphysical theology. To conceive the Deity as he is, we must conceive Him as first cause, as absolute and as infinite." (p. 44.) The spirit of this announcement, it seems to me, is not assuring ; not assuring especially, to those who feel that the discussion about to be entered upon touches a question of life and death to them, touches *the one*, most momentous point in the whole range of philosophy and theology. Withal I question whether it be actually true that these three terms *are* familiar as household words, in the vocabulary of philosophy. On the contrary, are they not among its highest and rarest symbols, and do they not belong to a profound, even inaccessible region? At all events, they certainly are meant to embody ideas which the lecturer holds to be altogether inconceivable. Fichte, Schelling, and Hegel in Germany, and Jouffroy and Cousin in France, have freely made use of the terms in question. But with the exception of Coleridge, they were all but entirely foreign to this country, till the appearance of Sir William Hamilton's celebrated review of Cousin's *Philosophy of the Infinite*, now thirty years ago. Even now, it seems scarcely becoming in any writer to boast of a household familiarity with words, which, though they have come into more general use, have not ceased to represent the highest and hardest abstractions of metaphysics.

It is no fault of the lecturer, but it is of some importance to bear in mind, that the argument which is forthwith constructed, in the second and third discourses, *the* portion of the work which is devoted to continuous reasoning, the other portions being more popular than argumentative, is substantially and virtually that of Hamilton's celebrated review. It is altered in some, even essential, respects, and it is greatly extended in parts, and many special additional details are introduced, but all the strongest points are contained, either expressly or implicity, in the earlier criticism.

One other thing must not be omitted in these preliminary notices ; the lecturer accepts, without a word of vindication, the distinction between the Infinite and the Absolute, which can rest only on the authority of Hamilton. Neither Kant, nor Fichte, nor Schelling, nor Hegel mark any noticeable difference in the meaning of these words. Etymologically they amount to much the same thing, and at least by the German metaphysicians they are used indifferently. Hamilton takes a course peculiar to himself, and constitutes the Unconditioned a genus, of which the Infinite and the Absolute are the species. Perhaps the exigencies of his system, and especially his favorite theory of causality, needed this distinction. At all events, for himself he selects the pair of contraries—an absolute whole, and an absolute part, a whole all inclusive, such that it cannot be conceived as part of a larger whole, a part so small that it cannot be conceived as a whole, capable of being again divided into parts—and gives to them the name of the Absolute, completed, finished, perfect, whole, *the unconditionally limited.* What is meant by the whole and the part, thus described, may be intelligible. But I am not ashamed to confess that, when this is called the unconditionally limited, I do not understand the words nor do I believe that they are capable of being understood by any person. To me, they are not sense, as little so, as would be the expression, solidly liquid, or coldly hot. Unconditionally limited ! The first term is directly contradictory of the second. At all events, it was not justifiable, even in Sir William Hamilton, that a formula, *at least* apparently contradictory, should be noted by him as the Absolute ; that is to say, should usurp for its own use a term already occupied, quite in a different sense—namely, as synonymous with the Infinite. But yet less justifiable is it in the Bampton lecturer to take up the supposed distinction between the Infinite and the Absolute, as if it were universally admitted, especially since, as we shall presently find, he had not even Hamilton's ground for making any distinction at all. And he does all this, with Mr. Calderwood's very noticeable book, to which he expressly refers, before him, containing, as it does, an ingenious and robust exposure of Hamilton's use of the terms in question.* The lecturer, it seems to me, was scarcely entitled in these circumstances to pass on in simple silence : and until the opposing reasonings be set aside—and I believe they cannot be set aside—we must regard *the unconditionally limited*, that is, the Absolute, as distinguished from the Infinite, as a palpable blunder.

---

* *The Philosophy of the Infinite*, by Henry Calderwood—a very rare example of early power and promise, which would have done honor to a ripe and practised metaphysician.

But the extraordinary fact is, that while the lecturer resolves to distinguish the Infinite from the Absolute, he does not use the latter term in Hamilton's sense at all, though this be *the only sense*, which makes it, however, strangely and contradictorily, distinguishable from the Infinite. In a note on his second lecture, he tells us, " the other sense in which the Absolute is contradictory of the Infinite, is irrelevant to the present argument." (p. 301.) But Hamilton says, " in *this* acceptation,"—he means, *as contradictory* of the Infinite —" for myself, I exclusively use it,"—the term Absolute (p. 13.) *The* meaning which the lecturer attaches to the Absolute is the very one which it never bears in Hamilton's use of the word ; namely, " aloof from relation, comparison, limitation, condition, dependence," etc., and it is thus, says Hamilton, tantamount .to τὸ ἀπολύτον of the lower Greeks. In *this* meaning," he adds, *i. e., the* meaning selected by the Bampton lecturer—" the Absolute is not opposed to the Infinite."* It *is* not indeed, it is not even distinguishable from it. For how better could we define the Infinite, than in the very words here employed to define the absolute, " aloof from relation, comparison, limitation, condition, dependence," etc. Absolute, *i. e.*, absolved, loosed, freed from—what ? connections, relations, boundaries, limits, without limits, infinite. The

* *Discussions*, p. 13.

two words are virtually identical, and only an imagined imperious necessity, which in this case is certainly not shown, can account for the abortive attempt to distinguish between them. It is possible to detect the merest shade of difference, when the lecturer says, " by the Absolute is meant that which exists in, and by itself, having no necessary relation to any other being. By the Infinite is meant that which is free from all possible limitation, that than which a greater is inconceivable." (p. 45.) But we can perceive in a moment that the definitions might be reversed with perfect justice. Quite as truly it might be asserted that the Infinite, like the Absolute, is that which exists in, and by itself, and which can have no necessary relation to any other being. On the other hand, quite as truly, so far as yet appears, it might be asserted that the Absolute, like the Infinite, is that, than which a greater is inconceivable, and which is free from all possible limitation. " Aloof from limitation," etc., is Sir William Hamilton's very phrase. The Absolute, at all events in the lecturer's sense of the word, and the Infinite, are identical, and yet he distinguishes them, as if they were perfectly different, and as if the difference were universally understood and admitted. Hamilton had a reason in the exigencies of his system for distinguishing between the two terms, and he constructed a defence of the distinction, however insufficient, and even contradictory. The lecturer does not give any reason, and does not make any defence. I am unable to conjecture why he employed two hard, uncouth, and, as he believes, unintelligible words, when one might have sufficed ; why, especially, he imposed two separate definitions which were both distinctly contained in either of the two terms. But I am obliged to own that in the circumstances an anticipative distrust of his accuracy, and of the soundness of his reasoning is created in my mind.

CHAPTER II.

UP to a certain point, there can be little difference one would imagine ; *there is* in fact, little difference, amongst moderate men, of however opposite schools, as to the at least apparent contradictions in which reason is involved, when it attempts to construct *a philosophy* of the Infinite or Absolute. Most would agree—*do* in fact agree—though this is very far from the impression suggested in the Bampton Lecture—that there is so much of inscrutable mystery in the region of the Divine, so much that is necessarily incomprehensible, that anything approaching to a *system*, a fully comprehended and explained philosophy, with the ground principles on which it rests, is never to be reached. The grand error—but not of extreme rationalists, at least, not of them only—of theologians, is, that they have philosophized too much, and not well ; that they do philosophize, philosophize falsely, and profess to give forth a round whole of religious truth, a completed scheme which leaves comparatively little unexplained. It cannot be. Hints *towards* such an issue, more or less inspiring and precious, may be possible; occasional gleams in one direction and another, openings into the deep unknown, the recovery here of one patch of surface hitherto dark, and there of another, and bringing them within the range of the light, may be possible. But anything approaching to a complete philosophy of the Infinite, or a philosophy of religious truth, natural or revealed, few will hesitate to pronounce a mere imposibility. But many who would readily make this admission, shrink back from such conclusions as those of the Bampton lecturer, and especially from his (as I judge) not satisfactory method of supporting them.

The second lecture in the series which is before us, is distinguished by high and hard abstractions, and by uncouth words, with the use of which few could boast a household familiarity. Our first business must be to pierce, as far as we are able, through the encrusting terms and forms, and to reach a meaning apprehensible by the common understanding. Scientific formulæ are unavoidable in marking scientific distinctions. But we deal here with spiritual truth; and whatever value there may be in the use of abstract terms, they are never, if they be really worth anything, incapable of being translated, it may be circuitously and cumbrously, into the ordinary language of thought. If they are untranslatable, it is because there is nothing to translate.

I have only further to submit, that with "*the* Absolute" of Schelling or Hegel, with the Unconditioned, the Absolute, the Infinite of German, or French philosophy I am not here to deal at all ; but only with these terms, as defined, explained, and reasoned upon in the Bampton Lecture ; and any argument of mine must be held to be valid, so long as it is soundly based only on these definitions, explanations, and reasoning.

The lecturer's first distinct position, as I gather, amounts to this, that the Infinite must be endowed with infinite attributes, and that their number must be infinite. Passing by the contradiction involved in the idea of an infinite number, it must be borne in mind that we have nothing to do with the relevancy, as respects the general argument, of this or of any of the other positions maintained. Taking them as they stand, I am only concerned to show, by one or two examples, the inexact nature of the reasoning. "The Infinite," I quote from lecture second, "cannot be regarded as consisting of a limited number of attributes, each unlimited in its kind. It cannot be conceived, for example, after the analogy of a line infinite in length but not in breadth, or of a surface infinite in two dimensions of space but bounded in the third, or of an intelligent being possessing some one or more modes of consciousness in an infinite degree, but devoid of others." (p. 45.) The conclusion is,—or if not, what is it?—that the Infinite must possess infinite attributes and an infinite number of them. What then, one might ask? The use to be made of such a conclusion, supposing it reached, and its precise effect on the general argument, it would be hard indeed to determine.

We shall meet with other examples of the evil and danger of such illustrations, borrowed from material nature, as occur in the passage just quoted, by which the highest spiritual truth is entangled and darkened. Here, however, even the illustration might have served to correct the statement, and ought to have suggested that what might seem limitation in the number of attributes may be only a mere necessary fact, an addition being simply impossible, in the nature of things. Suppose a body infinite not in two dimensions only, but in all three alike; it could then be infinite in no other, for no other is possible. Length, breadth, and thickness comprise the dimensions possible to extended body. Any other, according to our modes of judging, is impossible in the nature of things.

It must be noticed emphatically, that there is a

vast distinction, which is thoroughly overlooked by the lecturer not in this place merely, but throughout the entire discussion, and the overlooking of which necessarily creates confused and fallacious reasoning. It is the distinction, between a *supposed* quantitative Infinite, and *the* qualitative Infinite. Let the notion be attempted, however vain, of "The Infinite Whole"—a quantity, an amount, including everything, to which nothing by possibility can be added, and from which nothing by possibility be subtracted. *This* Infinite—if a fiction so baseless may be suffered to keep itself, for a moment, before our imagination—is strictly one, and there *can* be nothing besides. This is *the* Infinite (if you will), and there can be nothing but this Infinite. It can admit of no parts. Partition is at once destructive of the conception, or rather the fiction. Distinct, separate personality is impossible ; distinct, separate qualities or attributes are impossible. But the *qualitative* Infinite involves no such necessary results. *An* Infinite, as to duration, does not render a finite, as to duration—which is another and separate thing—impossible to our thought. Without contradiction, the two may co-exist. So also distinct and separate personality is not here swallowed up and lost, as in the One Infinite. *An* Infinite Being—quite remote from the notion of a quantity, an amount, to which nothing can be added without destroying it—does not render the existence of a finite being or of finite beings impossible to our thought. Without contradiction, they may co-exist. Even beyond this, an Infinite attribute does not render another distinct and different Infinite attribute, or many distinct and different Infinite attributes, impossible to our thoughts.

The fancied, *quantitative* Infinite is One, and there can be nothing besides. All parts, all personalities, all separate qualities are necessarily merged and lost in it. But with the notion of the *qualitative* Infinite, there may co-exist, without contradiction, as many Infinites as there are attributes. Knowledge and Power belong to spheres which interfere not in any possible way, the one with the other. They cannot come into collision. Without contradiction, Power may be unlimited and Knowledge may also be unlimited. Veracity, Rectitude, Love, and a thousand Infinites besides, co-existing at the same time, are not impossible to our thought.

To come more closely to the point from which we started, the difference is hardly to be estimated, when we pass from quantity to quality, from gross amount to attributes. Thus, it is no limitation of Unlimited Power that it is not Knowledge, and no limitation of Unlimited Knowledge that it is not Power. It is not in the nature of things, that these qualities should be interpenetrable or con-

vertible, and that the separate independent existence of the one should be incompatible with that
of the other. In like manner, in a lower sphere,
the sphere of the finite, it is no limitation to
mind, that it cannot walk, and no limitation to
truth or love, that you cannot measure them by a
scale of inches. These things are simply impossible. If then we say that the Infinite, as defined,
is necessarily endowed with all possible attributes
—this is the very utmost which the definition allows to be said. That all possible attributes make
up, and *must* make up an infinity ; this, true or
false, is at all events not shòwn. Take the writer's own illustration of " an intelligent being possessing certain modes of consciousness in an infinite degree," and say that in place of *certain*
modes the being possesses *all* the modes of consciousness possible to an intelligence ; can it be
maintained, besides, that these amount, and *must*
amount to infinity ? No man is entitled to advance such a position. It is utterly incapable of
proof. On the contrary, it is clear, if we suppose,
as the lecturer himself supposes, a purely spiritual
nature, there is at least one class of attributes,
those included in extension, which could have no
possible application to it. We come to this : the
attributes of a pure intelligence, each infinite in
kind, nevertheless could include—and this, without the slightest limitation of the Being—only so

much as was possible, in the nature of things : and whether this might or might not amount to infinity is a point unsettled.

Again : it is maintained that the Absolute must include in itself all being and all modes of being, actual and possible, not even excepting evil. There are two distinct applications of which these terms, the Infinite, the Absolute, are, or at least in this work are held to be, susceptible :—1st, to the one Absolute Being, God (the words are not mine ; I shall by and by try to show that they are false and contradictory). 2d, to the Whole, the all-inclusive Whole, without distinction of Divine or human, Infinite or finite, the All, the τὸ πᾶν of the early Greeks.

It is perplexing that the lecturer takes advantage of both of these senses, and passes them inexplicably from one hand to the other, of course undesignedly, but never keeps fixedly to either. You have references that can apply only to " The One," and again, others that can apply only to " The All ;" but you have no security that the same application shall be retained in two successive illustrations. He turns from the one to the other without notice.

In the case immediately before us it is manifestly intended to convey that " The One," the Infinite, living Being, must include all existence, not even excepting evil. But it is overlooked that an antagonist has still the alternative of "The All," the all-inclusive Whole. *This* he might argue is *the* Absolute, and *this* contains in itself all actual modes of being and all possibility of being. But what then ? what is gained by the admission, the admission of a fact which nobody denies, however they may deal with it ? What is gained by it ? Nothing ; at least by the lecturer, in the present stage of his reasoning, literally nothing.

But it is argued farther, not only that the Infinite or Absolute must contain in itself all actual being, but that all actual being must contain the realization of every possible mode of being. "The entire distinction," he says, "between the possible and the actual can have no existence as regards the absolutely Infinite, for an unrealized possibility is necessarily a relation and a limit." (p. 46.) The Infinite, as here conceived and represented, has reached its last development—has had its utmost possibility actualized, and has become one vast, boundless monotony, over which no breath of change can ever pass ; a gross, gorged, dead complement of being, to which movement of any sort, even from within, is for ever denied. *This* surely is limitation, iron necessity, for ever bounding and crushing all existence, not only not involved in the idea of *the* Infinite, or rather, of an infinite, but opposed to it : *this* is, if any thing can be, *the unconditionally limited*, entirely contradictory of the

Infinite, which sense, however, the lecturer has formally abjured.   But here it is.   The rationalist is justified in pronouncing all this a flat denial of the patent facts of nature.   The Great Whole, he could maintain, is the residence of forces that are ceaselessly in action ; of laws that ceaselessly reign in the harmony and order of the universe.   A pause in the action of these forces, in the reign of these laws, would be a limit to "The All" in the most direct, possible form.   Endless development and production resulting from power in harmony with law—in other words, the never-ceasing conversion of the possible into the actual—*this*, he might assert, constitutes the true and grand idea of the Infinite, The All.

But, as has already been noticed, the intended reference, in the passage we are examining, must certainly be not to "The Whole," the $\tau\grave{o}$ $\pi\grave{a}\nu$, though it is perfectly legitimate for an antagonist to resort to this alternative, but to The One ; for in confirmation or illustration of what had been advanced, a sentiment is introduced which can apply only to the One.   "The scholastic saying, '*Deus est actus purus*,' ridiculed as it has been by modern critics, is, in truth, but the expression in technical language of the almost unanimous voice of philosophy, both in earlier and later times." (p. 47.)   The saying in question, like many other aphoristic symbols of the schoolmen, contains a profound truth.

From all sides it cannot be accepted, but on some sides it is both true and grand. God is nobly conceived as everywhere, and ever, *in act*, a ceaseless, infinite energy. The duration of God the schoolmen represented as the "*punctum stans*," in which there could be no past, no future, no succession—an everlasting now. His *nature*, in certain essential aspects, they described when they said, " *Deus est actus purus*"—God is pure, mere, simple act ; the one all-pervading, living power of the universe ; unlabored, spontaneous, untiring, eternal, universal energy. But what has this to do with the necessity, which the lecturer seeks to make out, that all possible modes of being must also be actual, existing modes of being ? Nothing. So far from it, the adduced confirmation or illustration is the clearest possible refutation of his position. The idea of ceaseless action suggests that of ceaseless production, not the completed actualization of all possibilities, but never-ending conversion—an irrepressible, inner life, coming forth in ever new developments.

Meanwhile, it is certain that the lecturer, in the statement which he would confirm or illustrate by the quotation from Thomas Aquinas, had in his mind, not the All, but the One, the Infinite Being. In so many words, this is distinctly conveyed subsequently : " A mental attribute, to be conceived as infinite, must be in actual exercise on every possible object; otherwise, it is potential only with regard to those on which it is not exercised; and an unrealized potentiality is a limitation." (p. 51.) Were a mental attribute simply brute force, these • statements would be, at least, partially admissible. Brute force, left to itself, is not only necessarily in action, but necessarily in its utmost possible action, and on all objects on which it can bear. A steam power, whatever be its amount, goes forth to the limit of that amount, and on all objects belonging to its sphere, and within that sphere. Introduce the additional idea of mind, of reason, of will, of choice, and you have no longer an irresistible, brute necessity of action, but power commanded and regulated by its possessor, now let forth, or again held back. Is that a limit which substitutes choice for necessity? Is that a limit which elevates and extends power, and glorifies its possessor? But what can be meant when it is asserted, "if a mental attribute be not in actual exercise on every possible object, it is potential only with regard to those on which it is not exercised." This may not be, but it looks wonderfully like a contradiction. The only intelligible meaning which it can have is this, where an attribute has been actually exercised to its utmost limit, it is no longer potential, it is expended, exhausted. But where it has not been put forth, yet might be, it is still potential, it waits *to be* exercised. A potentiality realized is done with ; there is an end of it. *That*, surely, is a limit. But if so, what shall we say of its opposite ? Is it also a limit ? " An unrealized potentiality is a limit," says the lecturer. But power which is truly infinite, *must be* for ever un-- • realizable in its utmost extent, and *just because it is infinite.* Let the manifestations of it be ever so overwhelming, there must be a reserve of potentiality within and beyond, which can never be exhausted. If power in the Infinite is not put forth in every possible mode, so as to convert all possibility into actuality—in other words, if there is such a thing with the Great Being as unrealized potentiality ; this, so far from imposing a limit on his nature, so far from making it finite, is the very thing which we mean to convey when we say it is infinite.

Mr. Mansell proceeds—" hence," and yet, for one, I am quite unable to discover anything like a necessary, or even probable sequence—" hence, every infinite mode of consciousness must be regarded as extending over the field of every other, and their common action involves perpetual antagonism." (p. 51.) If we suppose a literal field, completely filled up by different bodies of solid, material actors, who have, at the same time, in the same space, different and conflicting sets of operations to carry forward, Mr. Mansell's difficulty would be realized. But spiritual powers do not occupy space, do not fill up space, so as to impede and obstruct action. Rectitude, and wisdom, and love, and truth, have perfectly different spheres belonging to them, though in the same mind, and cannot, by any possibility, come into material collision with one another. These perfections may be misused, either by not being sufficiently in exercise, or by being put forth wrongly. But spiritual attributes, extending over each other's fields, so as to impede each other's action, what can it mean ? I am unable to tell. It seems gross in idea, and not consistent with a belief in the essential distinction between matter and mind. But very noticeable is it, that this unhappy statement is scarcely sooner made, than the lecturer escapes from it—and to what ? to human sin, moral freedom, and the mysteries of providence, matters specially theological, even scriptural, far away from the high abstractions amidst which we have been soaring. Into this devious region we must not at present venture.

4*

CHAPTER III.

THE lecturer maintains (pp. 47–53) that the idea
of cause is contradictory of the idea either of The
Infinite or "The Absolute."

Dealing as he professes to do with the modern
forms of rationalism, he might have been expected
to notice that causation is entirely abandoned in
certain quarters, and that in its place we have the
forces and laws of the universe, and resulting from
them an eternal, infinite series of developments. It
might have been a well-timed and valuable service,
had he set himself to expose this subtle and spreading form of infidelity. Far better this, than to
expend time and power in laboriously and learn-
edly plucking to pieces what I humbly conceive no
party or school here is found to uphold ! Far better this, than, as I have striven to show and hope
still farther to show, to argue inconclusively against

a system which has next to no standing in this country, and is never in the least likely, judging by present appearances, to have a standing amongst us.

That there are profound mysteries surrounding the idea of creation, *of creation in time*, for that is the point, in the common form, in which it is put, and more, that the notion of *the* Infinite beginning to cause and giving being to a finite universe, is incapable of being grasped by the human mind, is most fully admitted. But, I must deny that the lecturer has touched the real difficulty. He has shown that the whole subject may be involved in the thickest darkness, and he has multiplied the contradictions and confusions to which, by one method of reasoning, it may lead ; but I must deny that even the extremest rationalists are without the means of replying successfully, at least, to much that he has advanced. Some of his reasonings, in my humble judgment, are very far from being conclusive.

" A cause," he says, " cannot as such, be absolute ; the absolute cannot, as such, be a cause." (p. 47.) Is one allowed to ask why? The thing is far from being self-evident. I maintain that his distinctly laid down definition of the Absolute contains nothing, at least palpably, inconsistent with the idea of cause. " That which exists in and by itself, and has no necessary relation to any other being"—for *so* the Absolute is defined—may, retaining all its self-sufficiency and absoluteness, have a voluntary, a self-imposed relation to other being. At least I am unable to perceive how this can be denied. It is freely granted, that very new and totally different ground is broken open, when it is added to the words already quoted : "on the other hand, the conception of the absolute implies a possible existence *out of all relation*." I simply call special attention to this short clause—it will be examined presently.

Meantime, the argument founded on it is, in so many words, Sir William Hamilton's, perhaps the very strongest which even he was able to produce. But I apprehend that its strength is his alone, and cannot serve his disciple in the slightest degree. 1st. Hamilton was contending against Cousin's theory, not of the Absolute, as cause, but of an absolute cause, a necessary, eternal cause, a cause which *must* pass into act. The precise words of Cousin are these—" The distinguishing characteristic (of God) being an absolute creative force, which cannot but pass into activity, it follows not that the creation is possible, but that it is necessary." The cause in Hamilton's reasoning is not the cause in Mr. Mansel's reasoning, but totally different ; and the argument, which is appropriate and powerful, if not invincible as applied to the one, loses all its point and force as applied to the other. 2d. The Absolute to which Hamilton refers is not the Absolute to which Mr. Mansell refers, but totally different, indeed diametrically opposite. "As contradictory of the Infinite," and in no other acceptation, Sir William Hamilton declares he invariably uses the term Absolute. But this sense the lecturer finds "irrelevant to his argument," and he has avowedly and formally adopted quite another; a sense in which the word "is not opposed to the Infinite," in which I have tried to show it is not even distinguishable from the Infinite, but is virtually and essentially the same. Bearing this in mind, how shall we interpret that short clause to which, a few moments ago, special attention was called? How shall we understand the words, "the conception of the Absolute implies a possible existence *out of all relation?*" No; "the Absolute," as deliberately and formally defined by the lecturer, implies no such thing, and he is guilty of uncommon carelessness in asserting that it does. The palpable logical blunder is so great and so serious in its consequences that it is scarcely pardonable. "The Absolute," in Sir William Hamilton's sense, *does* imply "a possible existence out of all relation;" but the lecturer distinctly abandons this sense, and as distinctly accepts another definition, which is purposely antagonistic to that of Hamilton. Indeed, as has been already noticed, Mr. Calderwood makes out the terms, Infinite and Absolute, to be

virtually synonymous, though, by a nice phraseology, it be possible to exhibit a slight shade of
difference in their signification. "By the Absolute," says Mr. Mansell, following Calderwood,
"is meant that which exists in and by itself, having no necessary relation to any other being." (p.
45.)   But, in the place of this, we find here the
important substitution, "the conception of the
Absolute implies a possible existence *out of all
relation.*"   It is glaringly in the face of his own
definition !   "*Out of all relation?*"   No, by no
means ; for the Absolute, as defined, is that which
has not no relation, but no *necessary* relation ;
and even more than this, no necessary relation *to
any other being.*   Two things are manifestly implied—1st. That external relation, and not internal, is contradictory of the Absolute, as he understands it.   2d. That even external relation is
contradictory, only if it be supposed to be also
necessary ; necessary, that is, to the very idea of
the being of the Absolute, so that it could not be
conceived apart from it.   Relation within itself is
admissible ; relation to other being is admissible,
provided always it be not necessary, not essential.
Temporary, incidental relation, voluntary self-imposed relation to other being is not contradictory
of the Absolute.   And yet we read, "the conception of the Absolute implies a possible existence
out of all relation."   It is not necessary to insist

further on this grave mistake ; but the lecturer *must* pardon his readers, if, after this, they greatly distrust his logical accuracy and precision.

The act of causation, it is further argued, must be voluntary ; volition is possible only in a conscious being, and consciousness supposes relation, at all events, between subject and object, the being choosing and the choice formed. With unnecessary amplification, it is said, " there must be a conscious subject and an object of which he is conscious. The subject is a subject to the object, and the object is an object to the subject, and neither can exist by itself as the Absolute." (p. 48.) But why not ? I am entitled to suppose by the Absolute what Mr. Mansell designates *The Absolute God*, and so much the more, indeed necessarily, because the argument respects *the act* of causation. An act supposes an actor. Now the relation between the Divine Mind and its conscious thought is purely internal, and internal relation was implied in the definition with which the argument set out. Are we again to find a logician not supplementing, but subverting his own definition and arguing against it ? We are. The lecturer does this, but without the least intimation that he is changing his ground. "The alternative (*i. e.*, of internal relation), he says, is, in ultimate analysis, no less self-destructive than the other. For the object of consciousness, whether a mode of the subject's

existence or not, is either created in and by the act
of consciousness, or it has an existence independent
of it. In the former case, the object depends on
the subject, and the subject alone is the true Absolute." (p. 49.) Of course it is, an antagonist might
reply, and stop him just at this point ; the subject
is the true Absolute—and what then ? We need
not go further. The other alternative proposed,
or any possible alternative besides, is not required.
This is enough. Of course the conscious subject
is the Absolute, if there be an absolute, and his
conscious choice is a mode of his existence. Substance and mode are not contradictory, but essen-
tial·the one to the other. And yet this is all, by
which the lecturer seeks to subvert his own definition, and feels himself entitled to assert, " Not
only is the Absolute, as conceived, incapable of a
necessary relation to anything else, but it is also
incapable of containing, by the constitution of its
own nature, an essential relation within itself."
Stop, an antagonist might say ; prove it ; the contrary is distinctly conceded in your own definitions—" as a whole, for instance, composed of
parts, or as a substance, consisting of attributes,
or as a conscious subject in antithesis to an object."
(p. 49.) I can only offer a direct negative to this
affirmation. It is not only not proved, I hold it
to be not true, to be the very contrary of the truth—
always taking the lecturer's own formal definition

of the Absolute as the legitimate one. Being
without attributes is a contradiction, an absurdity;
and no relation can be more indubitable, direct and
close, than that between being and its attributes.
It is essential, it is inevitable. It does not limit,
it constitutes being. Consciousness in like manner
is the condition of intelligence. Self-conscious intelligence is alone intelligence. I know that I
know, else I do not know at all. Intelligence
without self-consciousness is a nonentity, a purely
baseless idea.

The lecturer returns to the notion of Cause and
its incompatibility with that of either the Infinite,
or the Absolute. Much is made of the familiar
common-places, about creation involving a change
to the Creator, either from worse to better, or from
better to worse, from a lower to a higher, or from
a higher to a lower mode of being, or from one
state to another, the change being purely indifferent. On all which, for my part, I do not feel
called upon to say one word—inasmuch as the
same things advanced by infidels of different
schools, have been met, so far as they can be met,
many times over. This newer scepticism—for such
essentially I hold it to be, of course without the
remotest suspicion of the lecturer's personal faith
—contains only the old poison not even changed
in form. But how, it is asked, can the Absolute
give origin to the relative, the Infinite to finite?

We cannot tell, an extreme rationalist shall reply, and as little can you tell, and yet you believe it. It is incomprehensible to us, as it is to you, and not more. The alternative is before us—either matter is eternal or the one Infinite Intelligence caused the universe of matter and mind. We cannot comprehend this, and you cannot comprehend it. We cannot interpret either the fact or the mode or the time of creation, and you cannot interpret these. But *we* believe in the creation, and you having no other evidence than is open to us, believe in it. Believing in it, we defy any one to prove that it is contradictory. To the power of the Infinite Being, we like you, can affix no limits. New developments of that power are ever to be expected. They can neither create nor exhibit change in Him, but are only fresh forms of expressing what He is, what He immutably, eternally is.

" But how," asks the lecturer, " can the relative be conceived, as coming into being ? If it is a distinct reality from the Absolute, it must be conceived as passing from non-existence into existence." " To think of an object in the act of becoming, in the progress from not being into being, is to think that which in the very thought annihilates itself." (p. 53.) It is enough to reply, that there can be *no such progress*, and it is not imagined that there can be, as the lecturer describes, no such *act of becoming, no such passing* from non-existence into existence, *no such coming* into being. What is really supposed or imagined is this : One instant, the Infinite Being is alone; besides Him, there is absolutely nothing. The next instant, something else is, the creation is. It is, that is all we can say. It has not *come*, as from one place to another. It is. It has not *passed*, as from one state to another. It was not. It is. It has not *become* anything, having been something else before. It simply is. It has not made *progress* by a single step. It never was anything, anywhere. It is. That is all we can say. How it is, or why, or why not earlier, or later, we cannot comprehend or explain. The lecturer asserts, but he has failed to prove, does not even attempt to prove, " the impossibility of conceiving the coexistence of the Infinite and the finite." On the contrary, it is the Being of a God, of an Infinite, which make the patent, admitted fact of the existence of the finite—at least to many minds—either intelligible or credible.

Just as little can we acknowledge " the cognate impossibility of which he speaks, of conceiving a first commencement of phenomena or the absolute giving birth to the relative." (p. 54.) We have here the one fatal error in Sir William Hamilton's system, as some of its devoutest disciples confess with sorrow, the true origin of whatever else is objectionable in it. With something like infatuation that great man, betrayed by fondness for his own theory of causation, clung to the idea of " the impossibility of conceiving an absolute commencement or an absolute termination." The question of the conceivability of the idea of the Infinite is here quite apart, the question of the comprehensibility of the fact or the mode of creation is also quite apart. All that is at issue, is simply this : When the statement is made, " this instant God is alone, besides Him there is absolutely nothing, the next instant something else is, creation is," does consciousness declare or does it not declare this absolute commencement of the finite to be inconceiveable, because contradictory ? Mr. Mansell, following Hamilton, maintains that it does. Many even of Hamilton's disciples, amongst whom I humbly claim to number myself, maintain that it does not. Authority, of course, goes for nothing in such a case. Calmly, profoundly, continuously meditating, divesting ourselves, in all honesty, of every prejudice and every prepossession, each must determine this question for himself. No authority, however justly venerated, can be suffered to suggest or supply what can have no value, unless it be the clear testimony of our own minds. For my part, I am as thoroughly satisfied as I can be of anything, that I *can* and *do* think, represent to myself, in thought, this first commencement of relative phenomena, and without the slightest sense of contradiction. The power which caused it is incomprehensible. The mode in which this power operated is also incomprehensible. But the effect of creative power, in the absolute commencement of new existence, I *can* and *do* think, I can and do represent it to my mind, without the slightest sense of contradiction. The idea of creation—and this, be it noted, is a much wider thing, and even perfectly different from *the* creation, the actual new existence, first beginning to be—is not contradictory. It has never been shown —we maintain it cannot be shown—to be contradictory. The lecturer asserts that it is,.but he has not proved his assertion.

Those who have concurred in the principles which I have sought to establish, in opposition to his reasoning, will agree with me, that it is not here only he has failed, but also in several of the conclusions which he sums up, towards the close of his second lecture. To one and another of these conclusions, be they true or false in themselves, I have to offer, so far as his arguments are concerned, a direct negative, on the ground of evidence already advanced. "The conception," says the lecturer, professing to sum up his reasonings thus far, but in reality not doing so, "of the Absolute and the Infinite, from whatever side we view it, appears encompassed with contradictions. There is a contradiction in supposing such an object to exist, whether alone or in conjunction with others, and there is a contradiction in supposing it not to exist. There is a contradiction in conceiving it as one, and there is a contradiction in conceiving it as many. There is a contradiction in conceiving it as personal, and there is a contradiction in conceiving it as impersonal. It cannot, without contradiction, be represented as active, nor, without equal contradiction, be represented as inactive. It cannot be conceived as the sum of all existence, nor yet can it be conceived as a part only of that sum." (p. 59.)

This peroration is unusually imposing, and is very admirably put. But it appears to me to have one fundamental and fatal fault, as we may discover, I humbly conceive, on casting our thoughts back on the course of the argumentation. It puts forward, in strong relief, propositions strikingly antithetical and telling in their sequence, but it does not contain the actual findings, and only the actual findings which appear in the body of the lecture itself. By no means; and hence it is destitute of all value, save that of very fine writing, out of place. Against several clauses of this eloquent and ingenious summary, I have tried to make good my right to put—" not proven." True or false, at least " not proven."

CHAPTER IV.

INCONCEIVABILITY OF INFINITE.

Admit Facts, refuse Arguments — Nature of Consciousness — Equivocal Limitation—Infinite, Finite—Distinction, just and real—Confusion—Inconsequent Reasonings—Consciousness of Infinite Contradictory?—Virtual Scepticism—Natural Theism Impossible?—This Inconsistent with Facts—Impeachment of the Almighty.

HAPPILY, it will not be necessary much longer to employ the kind of reasoning to which it has hitherto been unavoidable to have recourse. There are very vital, home-coming questions awaiting discussion, and it is a trial of patience and spirit to be detained from these by what, did it not lie in the way of something far higher, one might be provoked to regard as mere logical sleight-of-hand. I must also own to a feeling of pain, that in a case where the Great Being, and the spirit of man, and the destiny of the universe were concerned, it should have been necessary to resort to the coldest and hardest forms of logic, the most impalpable of metaphysical abstractions, and the veriest subtleties and illusions of dialectics. The sense of duty must have been overwhelmingly imperative, to compel an earnest and true soul to endure the substitution of shadow for substance, of verbal mechanism for living energy, and of mere dialectic for stern reality.

There are high and noble uses of metaphysics, I believe ; there is an absolute necessity for the rigid philosophical treatment of subjects which belong to the true sphere of philosophy. But we must not forget that extensive acquaintance with the history and the materials of speculation, perfect facility in the use of logical forms, and familiarity, even household familiarity, with the nomenclature of abstraction are not identical either with a true philosophic spirit or with sound reasoning, or with the maintenance of great and just principles. I have already tried to show, and I am about to produce still farther proofs, that the Bampton Lecture, justly celebrated on many accounts, is not a safe guide, either in philosophy or in theology, is not accurate in its reasonings, and not philosophical in its conclusions and its spirit.

Only very briefly will it now be necessary to do this ; and so much the more, as in the special point. which is laboriously argued in the third lecture, I shall have, by and by, to express at least a qualified concurrence. But even where the conclusion may be limitedly true, I wish to show that the argumentation is, to some extent, vicious and invalid.

The point to be made out in the third lecture is, that the Infinite is inconceivable by the human mind, and the proof is derived from the nature of human consciousness. With the issue, its actual truth or falsehood, I am not now concerned. But the proof is, in my humble judgment, unsatisfactory in many respects, and is accompanied with statements not only not supported, but untenable. "To be conscious, we must be conscious of something, and that something can only be known as that which it is, by being distinguished from that which it is not. But distinction is necessarily limitation." (p. 70.) Why so? Do I limit *something*, when I say it is not nothing? In the sense of distinguishing, defining, determining, I do limit ; but in the sense of circumscribing, narrowing, making less or other than it is, I do not necessarily limit. All knowledge is essentially discrimination, distinction, the separation and differentiation of things. Do I necessarily impose a limit—except in an equivocal sense—on everything, *by simply knowing it?* If this were true, it must apply much beyond the human consciousness, it must reach to the divine. The Infinite God is a conscious being. Consciousness is the condition of all knowledge, exist where it may. "I know that I know, else I do not know at all," is true universally, without any possible exception. Divine, like human consciousness, implies distinction of one thing from another—differentiation—for that is equivalent to knowledge. But beyond this, and perhaps still more clearly decisive, the Infinite

Being is self-conscious, knows himself ; and does He, must He, by this knowledge limit his own nature? Even from this alone, we are entitled to assert, with confidence, that to discriminate, to distinguish, to know, to be conscious, is *not necessarily* equivalent to limitation, except in an equivocal sense.

Again : " the infinite cannot be distinguished, as such, from the finite, by the absence of any quality which the finite possesses, for such absence would be a limitation. Nor yet can it be distinguished by the presence of an attribute which the finite has not ; for, as no finite part can be a constituent of an infinite whole, this differential characteristic must itself be infinite, and must, at the same time, have nothing in common with the finite." (pp. 70, 71.) I understand by *the Infinite*, and have a right to understand, the one living God. The lecturer himself, again and again, so understands it ; and he cannot be suffered, because it may be necessary for his special purpose, to enforce —the rationalist may legitimately refuse him the right of enforcing—in this instance, another sense, and of taking refuge in *the Infinite, the All*—a mere ideal abstraction. He admits, as his own personal belief, and those with whom he is contending, are entitled to keep him to the admission of One Infinite Being, the Creator of the finite universe. It is a patent fact that we can, and do, distinguish this Infinite Being from finite beings. Whether we be able fully to conceive and comprehend the Infinite is not the question. But, as a matter of fact, thus far, at least, we can, and do go ; every intelligent man does distinguish the Infinite Being from finite beings and things, and in the very way which is pronounced in this passage to be impossible. What is more, we are perfectly certain that the distinction so made is thoroughly well-founded and real. We distinguish the Infinite, I. by the absence of a quality which the finite possesses—finity, limitation. But in sober earnest, the lecturer asserts, that thus discriminating, differentiating the Infinite, *by the absence of limitation*, we do *limit* Him. II. by the presence of an attribute which the finite has not—infinity, non–limitation. But, it is said, the differential characteristic must itself be infinite, and so can have nothing in common with the finite. Of course, so. It does not need to have anything in common ; just because, in this point, the two have nothing in common, the distinction between them is complete.

Among other inconsequent passages, as I deem them, the following may be selected—" a thing, an object, an attribute, a person, or any other term, signifying one out of many possible objects of consciousness, is, by that very relation, necessarily declared to be finite" (is the one Infinite Being, because there is a finite creation, and distinguished from it, *necessarily* declared to be finite ? does the writer deliberately mean so ?)   " An infinite thing, or object, or attribute, or person, is, therefore, in the same moment declared to be both finite and infinite."   (p. 90.)   Were there only the Infinite, in the pure pantheistic sense, the Quantitative Infinite, if we so speak, the One Whole, the τὸ πάν (a very different thing from the Qualitative Infinite), and nothing but the Infinite ; all phenomena, and all finity, being mere illusion, the passage we have quoted might stand.   But rationalists, in common with the lecturer, are not restricted from supposing One Infinite Being, and, besides Him, finite beings and things.   The co-existence of the One and the many they do not profess to explain, nor does he, but it is a fact, and they accept the fact, as he also does ; the natural reason accepts it ; and they defy him, or any one, to prove that it is contradictory.   Inexplicable they will allow it to be, but not contradictory—at all events, accepted on both sides.   Now will the lecturer maintain that, when it is asserted that, besides limited beings and things there is one Being who is not limited, " who is free from all possible (that is, as I understand, *necessary*) limitation, and than whom a greater is inconceivable "—for such is his own definition—this is limiting that Being ? The thing is surely preposterous. Will he, aside from the Schellingian and Hegelian abstractions, with which we have nothing to do, maintain that by predicating attributes of that Being, in other words, by conceiving Him to be being, and not nothing— for, being without attributes is a contradiction— we limit Him? The fact is, that in these lectures not only is One Infinite Being admitted, but it is distinctly argued that his attributes, like his nature, must be infinite. Let us then take forth a single attribute—power! What do I limit, when I say that this power is unlimited ; or, if you will, infinite? True, power is not everything, it is " *the All*," it is not THE Infinite. And if the lecturer is only showing the impossibility of *the* Infinite, the " τὸ πάν," with whom is he contending, for where is the rationalist, in this country, who maintains it? And, surely, a logician will not imagine that he has gained a victory over those who stand by his side and are glad to see him, contending against a position to which they are as thoroughly opposed as he can be. Human reason finds no contradiction, though it does find profound mystery in the unlimited power, unlimited wisdom, unlimited spiritual excellence of the Being whose nature is all unlimited.

The same Schellingian, Hegelian, or Spinozistic Infinite, is assailed in another passage. " The Infinite, if it is to be conceived at all, must be conceived as potentially everything, and actually nothing ; for, if there is anything in general which it cannot become, it is thereby limited ; and if there is anything in particular which it actually is, it is thereby excluded from being any other thing. But, again, it must also be conceived as actually everything, and potentially nothing ; for an unrealized potentiality is a limitation." (p. 71.) All this is literally assailing nothing. *The* Infinite, in this sense, the τὸ πάν, the universal substans, who adopts the idea ? And yet even here, the veriest pantheist, I am presumptuous enough to think, might silence the Bampton lecturer on his own ground, and might say, Yes, *the* Infinite is potentially everything, and actually everything. There is no unrealized potentiality. Everything possible *is ;* and there is nothing which *the* Infinite cannot become, for no actual thing more is possible. And what then ? the pantheist might ask.

It is wearisome, lowering, and almost corrupting, this mere vaporing of words and forms of attack and of fence, which means nothing and can end in nothing, save that it must have a mischievous moral effect, alike on the writer and his readers.

I shall only notice, further, the form in which the lecturer puts the conclusion, when he thinks he has established "a consciousness of the Infinite, as such, thus necessarily involves a self-contradiction." (p. 71.) And yet a consciousness of the Infinite

God, a consciousness that the Infinite God exists, is vehemently maintained by Sir William Hamilton, and is again and again admitted in the Bampton Lecture. The incongruity is owing entirely to that illogical and (in effect) immoral shifting and shuffling of *the* Infinite and *an* Infinite, to which I have before had to refer. Here, "a consciousness of *the Infinite* is self-contradictory." But the writer can, when necessary, find Infinity in one living Being. "We are compelled," he says, "by the constitution of our minds, to believe in the existence of an Infinite and Absolute Being—a belief which appears forced on us, as the complement of our consciousness of the relative and the finite. But the instant we attempt to analyze the ideas thus suggested to us, in the hope of attaining to an intelligible conception of them, we are, on every side, involved in inextricable confusion and contradiction." (p. 68.) No, we are not, it might be replied; it is not true; unless, indeed, instead of keeping by the idea of One Infinite God, we shift it, ever and again, and substitute for it, *the* Infinite —a mere abstraction, a perfectly wild and unmeaning abstraction, against which it is utterly worthless labor for this accomplished writer to argue; for where is it held, where is anything approaching it held? "So long as human consciousness,"— these also are the words of the Bampton Lecture; with what consistency they are introduced any one may judge—"*contains* the idea of a God"—and He is *the* Infinite—"and the instincts of worship, so long mental philosophy will walk on common ground with religious belief." (p. 32.)

I think I may appeal to every reader of the work, whether, not the tendency, but one great and avowed purpose of it be not to separate mental philosophy from religious faith, to show that they are irreconcileable, and that faith has no security, save in a universal protest against the authority of the understanding. Again, "It is by consciousness alone, that we know that God" (and He is the Only Infinite) "exists, or that we are able to offer Him any service." (p. 86.) And yet the same writer maintains "that a consciousness of the Infinite (who is God) is self-contradictory," and, therefore, I should presume to argue, impossible.

Minute criticism of these two Lectures need not be pursued further. Looking back, especially to the second, and to the long array of contradictories, which is there slowly and formally drawn out, it is hardly possible to avoid thinking that, throughout, there is, at least, *seeming* satisfaction, in darkening and blasting what many regard as the natural beliefs and hopes of men. The irrepressible feeling in my mind—of course without for an instant impeaching the personal convictions of the writer, and referring solely to the reasonings and conclusions of his book—is, that I have been dealing with a virtual scepticism ; with a scepticism, moreover, which *seems* to gloat over its own blindness, and impotence, and degradation, and almost to exult in putting out its own eyes, and covering itself with shame and rags !

Theism, on the mere ground of our rational nature, and in the absence of written revelation, is impossible ! *That* is the conclusion which the Lecturer announces. The co-existence of the Infinite and the finite involves endless contradictions. Either we must abandon the finite and hold by the Infinite, adopting the scheme of Pantheism, or we must abandon the Infinite and hold by the finite, adopting the scheme of Atheism. But both alternatives alike land us in contradictions as great or greater than those from which we seek to escape. Theism, Pantheism, Atheism are impossible, nearly equally impossible ! Man cannot even read the alphabet out of which a rational Theism must be framed. Paragraphs, sentences of profound meaning, are impossible ! Even single words, the symbols of living ideas, precious as suggestive of undying truth, are impossible. Man is ignorant of the very letters of the alphabet, cannot join them together, cannot pronounce them, and cannot form even a solitary term.

It is a terrible conclusion, if it be true. But is it true ? Is it true that in the absence of written revelation, natural Theism is impossible ? Is it consistent with facts ?   Is there no Theist, has there never been a natural Theist, save among Jews or Christians ?   What of Mohammedans ?   Has no single soul, over all the ages, and in all the pagan world, amidst many darknesses, and inconsistences, and false beliefs, yet adhering to it,—has no single soul ever struggled up through the crowd of inferior divinities, to the idea and the faith of one Supreme Being ?   Has there been no Pythagoras, no Xenophanes, no Parmenides, no Socrates, no Plato, no Zeno, no Epictetus ?   And have there been no obscure and unprivileged souls, of whose ruder faith these higher spirits may suggest the existence ?

When we return—as on the lecturer's principles we should be compelled to return—a decisive negative to these questions, it must surely be forgotten that for thousands of years from the creation, mankind did not receive the boon of a written revelation, as we understand it ; that with the exception of one small tribe of men, all the nations of the world were destitute of this boon till the coming of Christ ; that in the 1800 years that have elapsed since, only the few, compared with the vast masses of the earth's population, have seen the light of the Christian Scriptures ; that at this moment, four-fifths of our race are in the midst of pagan or other darkness ; that under shelter of the name Christian, there are untold myriads who know nothing of these Scriptures—myriads who are even opposed to them. In consequence of their birth and education, over which they have had no control, owing to prejudiced and false notions which have been poured into them, not sought by them, they are ignorant of the New Testament and opposed to it. Is there no God to them? have they absolutely no means through the powers and tendencies of their own minds of reaching even to faith in God? Is there no God to all the outlying millions of our race? For 6,000 years or more, over all the world, has there never been a Supreme Being in the thought, in the heart of man, save among the few who have received a written revelation?

I hope I am profoundly thankful for the light of Christian truth, and do fervently long for its diffusion over the whole world. But among the teachings of the New and of the Old Testament I regard *this* as not the least divine, that the Great Father since the beginning of the world has been very near to the minds He has made, though they were neither Jews nor Christians; has ever had a witness for Himself within them; and, above all, has never ceased, by his Spirit, to strive with their evil, in order to subdue and cast it out, that they might be restored to Him, and might know and trust Him for ever.

CHAPTER V.

MISCELLANEOUS REASONINGS.

"Infinite," " Absolute," held equivalent to God—Conclusions as
to these applied to this—Investigation of Principles declared
wrong—Cannot reach Principles—Content with Regulations—
Truth and Falsehood—Properties of our Conceptions—Hume
and Berkeley—" Mind cramped by own Laws "—Unmitigated
Scepticism—Inconsistency of Reasoning—Suicidal.

IN the first of the Bampton Lectures a singular
quotation from Clemens Alexandrinus is introduced with at least qualified approbation. "It
has been actually said," writes the lecturer, " that
even if philosophy is useless, it is still useful as the
means of proving its own uselessness." Wherein
the acuteness of this saying lies it might be difficult to discover ; but certainly the Greek father
who uttered it must have lost all *his* faith in philosophy before he could think of exalting it to the
honor of proving its own uselessness. And the
modern lecturer, who appreciates the sharpness of
the Alexandrian salt, can hardly himself be a very
serious or determined believer. This little sentence at the outset is startling—almost suspicious.
What is to be expected from one who, about to
discuss, on the ground of philosophy, a high, and

sacred, and most momentous subject, betrays that he has little or no confidence in the instrument he is to employ? Nor has there been anything to quiet this early suspicion, so far as we have yet gone. Rather otherwise. Had the lecturer undertaken to show, he could have adopted no more effectual method than he has done of showing the utter uselessness and mischievousness of philosophy. The never-varying tendency of his work, I humbly conceive, is to destroy all respect for philosophy and for the efforts of human intelligence. So many things, it has been proved or attempted to be proved, philosophy cannot do, the human mind cannot do, that one is fain to inquire at this stage, is there anything which they *can* do? Where is this process of nullifying and annihilating to stop? Limits of religious thought! Doubtless, religious thought has its limits, and it must be important to discover them. But it must also have its sphere; and where is this? Here we have all limits together, on this side, on that side —nothing but limits everywhere. Difficulty is added to difficulty; the circumscribing cord is drawn tighter and tighter, narrower and narrower, until literally no atom of free space is left.

One who has been well nigh overwhelmed by the contradictions and confusions that are here so laboriously piled up, and who at first sees no escape from them, may be imagined to stop the lec-

turer and to ask tremblingly, before yielding himself without reserve—"But what more ? where is
this to end, or has it an end?   You tell me the
Infinite is inconceivable, and that a consciousness
of it is self-contradictory, and that the human
mind can do nothing towards solving the problem
of the universe—cannot work out for itself even a
single first principle—but what then ?   Whither
is this philosophical nihilism to conduct me ?
What more am I to be required to abandon ?   I
would see *the end ?*"

These questions are fair, and the answer which
they must receive is unmistakeable.   The lecturer
goes so far, and is so ingenuous, so explicit, that
doubt is impossible.   Hitherto the argument has
been restricted to *the* Infinite or Absolute, whether
One living Being, or a vast indefinite whole, or
both, is not determined, but, in any case, an idea
which it is possible to reach (if at all) only by
the highest effort of abstraction.   Throughout the
later lectures, however, the abstraction is dis-
missed, and by *the* Infinite or Absolute, the Divine Being is unmistakeably intended ; and what
had been proved, or supposed to be proved, in reference to the philosophical abstraction, is applied
to the only true God.   The lecturer began with
the position, that it is impossible to know *the Infinite;* he ends with the position, that it is impossible to know God—a somewhat different thing,

one might judge, and therefore a questionable conclusion, unless he has clearly shown that *the* Infinite or Absolute are convertible with God, and this he certainly has not done or professed to do. Meantime, it is again and again broadly asserted, that man does not and cannot know God; at all events, does not and cannot know that he knows God. The utmost, even with the aid of revelation, that we can reach is, " such a knowledge as is best adapted to our wants and training. But how far that represents God as He is, (I understand this to mean, how far it represents the true, the real God) we know not, and have no need to know." (p. 146.) It is explicitly declared, that "*the* Infinite (he means God, and can mean nothing else)—God—is not an object of human thought at all." (p. 218.) It is not yet the time, for showing all that must grow out of this conclusion, but it ought to be distinctly understood that on the principles of the Bampton Lecture it is not God, not very God, not the true God, but something essentially different from Him, and how far different we cannot ascertain, that we can ever know ; not God, not very God, not the true God, but something essentially different from Him, that we can ever worship.

Be it so—and what then ? It comes to this, at least, that only in some sphere, lower than the Divine—if at all—there can be scope for the efforts of the human mind. But even this hope is vain. The lecturer *distinctly aims* to make out that, within the entire range of speculative thought, there is nothing for us—at all events ultimately— but contradiction, confusion, and darkness. He states that the very first law of all thought and of all consciousness, the very first principle of action and feeling, and the very perception of our senses create for us only inscrutable mysteries. The understanding can do nothing, but blindly accept the conditions with which it is environed, or else stumble at the very first step into insoluble contradictions. Moral liberty, personality, individuality, and the commerce between mind and matter, stare us in the face, when we look out on the region of speculative thought, and vainly demand from us an interpretation. It cannot be given. The mere facts (of liberty, personality, etc.), the lecturer admits, are not inconceivable and not contradictory. So far from this, " they embody," he says, " the very laws of conception itself, and are experienced every moment as true." (p. 140.) But we must not speculate on them—it is impossible to gain the least satisfaction respecting them—all inquiry is not only useless, but wrong in its very principle. On every subject and on every side, the lecturer seems to be able only to heap up difficulties. The very things which are universally accepted and understood, he is at pains to show, are connected with others which are not understood at all, which cannot even be discovered. Any inquiry into these higher facts is peremptorily forbidden, as lying beyond the legitimate sphere of thought. At all events, " to such inquiry," he pronounces, " *no satisfactory answer can be given.*" (p. 141.) But surely, we may at the least try to advance, if but a step; we may patiently speculate, and pierce, and wait for light? No. At *this* point, without an effort to inquire, he would have us *rest!* But why? For a reason which is even more startling than the statement, for which it is supposed to account. " The highest principles of thought and action to which we can attain," he says, " are regulative, not speculative; they do not serve to satisfy the reason, but to guide the conduct." (p. 141.) The counter-assertion is enough; the highest principles *do* satisfy the reason, and they *then* best guide the conduct, when they have first satisfied the reason.

I cannot and will not argue such a point as this. But I may be suffered to ask, is this philosophy? —is this the spirit of philosophy?—has *this* been inspired by the writings of Sir William Hamilton? With a deeper feeling than I care to clothe in words, I answer—no, it has not; it is as wide as the poles asunder, from either the tone or the letter of the teaching of that great man. And I hope to furnish abundant proof of this, ere long. No :

the natural and true association of such ideas as
those just referred to is not with a high philosophy, but with a darkening scepticism.   Hence it is
no wonder to me, that the lecturer should find in
Hume—who, though perhaps personally not a
sceptic, made it the business of his life to show
that all philosophy and all speculative inquiry ter-
minated only in scepticism—I do not wonder that
the English logician should find, in the Scottish
sceptic, a statement, which in its letter and in its
aim, he can accept and commend.   "No priestly
dogmas," says Hume—I quote from the Bampton
Lecture, p. 138—"ever shocked common sense
more than the infinite divisibility of extension,
with its consequences.   He should have added,
that the antagonist assumption of a finite divisibility is equally incomprehensible."   Be it borne in
mind, that the substance of this statement is not the
question, respecting which men of the most opposite sentiments may concur; I refer to the sympathy of spirit between the sceptic and the logician,
at all events, to the oneness of tendency and effect
in their labors, to shock common sense, to put
down reason, and to beget scepticism.

Notwithstanding this, we are hardly prepared
for the assertion, in its stern dogmatic force, that
"truth itself is nothing more than a relation.
Truth and falsehood are not properties of things
in themselves, but of our conceptions .   .   .   .

truth, in relation to no intelligence, is a contradiction in terms." (p. 149.) It is quite admitted that our conceptions of things may be true or false; truth and falsehood *are* qualities of our conceptions. But are they *only* qualities of our conceptions? that is the question. A statement, a representation, a fact so-called, a principle, may be true or false in itself. Our idea of it is one thing, but its own actual, positive truth or falsehood is quite another thing. I am not ignorant how such positions as the lecturer's may be defended, in what logical forms they may be put and held to be invincible. But I know also that they are the very foundation of the idealism of Berkeley, of which, the idealism of Hume was the necessary and native consequence, and I hold them to be as ruinous as they are unsound.

Perhaps it ought not to be matter of surprise that the writer, who has evidently lost faith in the human mind, and certainly aims to destroy its authority, and can be satisfied with nothing short of its utter humiliation, should also be doubtful respecting truth itself, should question its independent reality, and should reduce it to a mere modification of the conscious subject, a mere quality of our conceptions. Happily, there is an untaught dialectic, in this case, a native, instinctive logic which is more than a match for all the subtlety of the schools. The common sense, I mean *communis*

sensus, in the old, high signification, the common
reason of men rebels against this idealistic theory,
and will have none of it. There *is* such a thing as
truth ; there *are* such things as truths, independent
realities, apart from our conceptions altogether, be
they right or wrong. Immortality, responsibility,
are real properties of beings, not mere subjective
affections. Wisdom, rectitude, purity, benevolence,
are real properties of beings in themselves, independent, immutable entities attaching to substance,
and not essentially affected by any conceptions that
may be formed in any mind concerning them.
These conceptions may be true, and they may be
false, they may vary endlessly ; but truth and
truths are immutably, eternally the same.

In connection with the principles that have now
been instanced, the Bampton lecturer seems to narrow the compass, and to enfeeble the intellectual
power of man, to an extent, and with an undis-
guisedness, which are somewhat confounding. He
seems desirous of encompassing this part of our
nature with difficulties which it cannot remove,
and with darkness which it cannot penetrate, and
of showing that it has, and can have no other inheritance than this. "Such problems"—he means
problems insoluble—"arise inevitably, whenever
we attempt to pass from the sensible to the intelligible world, from the sphere of action to that of
thought, from that which *appears* to us, to that

which *is*, in itself." (p. 135.) Where then, any one may now ask, is the sphere of human intelligence ? We can only answer, nowhere ; for the intelligible world, the world of thought, the world of reality, in distinction from that of phenomena, is shut against us. Where is the sphere of human intelligence, as an essential part of our mental constitution ? nowhere. It has no sphere, unless we accept from the lecturer the world of sense, of action, and of outward phenomena, the same over which the bodily senses and the animal instincts, and the mere calculating, prudential faculty, preside. It is impossible that anything can be more unqualified, undisguised, and free, than the language in which our destiny is pronounced. " In religion, in morals, in our daily business, in the care of our lives, in the exercise of our senses, the rules which guide our practice cannot be reduced to principles which satisfy our reason." (p. 135.)

Emphatically and utterly I protest against this view of human experience. It is not consistent with fact. It is wholly at variance with fact. Were it meant, that we cannot reach principles, which leave no unanswered question behind, *this* would be quite admissible, and since the range of truth is unlimited, this must also apply to intellects higher far than the human. Even they cannot advance to the utmost boundary of truth and of knowledge, beyond which no question can arise.

But apply where it may, this is not what is stated, but something essentially different. And if what is stated be really meant, that we cannot reach principles, which, whatever questions they leave behind, are nevertheless satisfactory to the reason, I answer, this is contradictory to all fact. The distinction is acknowledged every day, and is patent to all, between those who merely follow practical rules, and those who search into the principles on which the rules are based. The one form the class of prudent, correct, successful persons. The latter are distinctively called wise. In religion and morals, the mere servants of custom and of precepts are, at the best, decent, harmless, innocent. They, on the other hand, who inquire, and investigate, and search for the grounds of religious belief, and of moral law, until they are able to satisfy their rational and their moral nature, only they are really virtuous and pious. In the actual experience of life, persons in whom the trust of their fellow-creatures is reposed are such as are believed to have thought for themselves, and made their deliberate election of principles, and come to a fixed purpose to stand by them, at all hazards. For the individual self, there is no inward rest, and no real strength to suffer or to do, save from deep, satisfying, immovable convictions. "Men of principle"—in distinction from mere practice—is not a flourish of words, a poor deception which we put upon ourselves, in order to conceal an unwelcome fact. There is a reality answering to it! There is such a thing as examining, discovering, and laying hold of deep and sure principles, which in their measure, satisfy the reason, and are felt to be indestructible.

Were the representations, from the Bampton Lecture, which have been produced, true, then for once, we might altogether agree with the lecturer in the method by which he accounts for them. They would verily suggest—he distinctly says, and believes they do suggest, and he puts it as the actual fact of the whole case—" they suggest, as their obvious explanation, the hypothesis of a mind cramped by its own laws, and bewildered by the contemplation of its own forms." (p. 142.) These are his very actual words, and to me, *this* conclusion—of course, referring solely to the book, and not questioning for a moment, the actual personal convictions of the writer—seems the climax of an unmitigated scepticism! In my humble judgment, it is blasphemy against human reason! blasphemy against the Being who formed the mind of man! Aye! its Father! God is the Creator of all things, but he is the Father of minds, *only* of minds, *but* of minds. And what of his child—the mind of man? Here is the answer of the lecturer, " a cramped, bewildered thing, cramped by its own laws, bewildered in its own forms !"   It can avail him nothing, to take refuge in the doctrine of the fall, or of original sin.   *He* blasphemes the very primitive constitution of the mind, the original laws, the essential thought-forms, established by The Maker, and he declares that they can terminate—are designed to terminate, save within the sphere of the senses—though even here, one cannot forget that he has said that the very perception of our senses creates for us insoluble mysteries—in nothing but contradiction, confusion, and darkness.   One of the grossest paradoxes of Germany has been outdone here in England.   For what end were eyes given ?   To limit vision, was the reply of the German sage.   But here,—for what end was mind given ? to limit knowledge, to prevent us from knowing, to cramp and bewilder the being endowed with it.

In the presence of such, or anything approaching such an announcement, I think of ingenuous, open, youthful souls !   By all means let them be warned against the danger of presumptuous and rash philosophizing.   But can we not also quicken and kindle them ?   Can we not touch their spiritual nature, with a wise and gentle hand, so as to awaken a tremulous response ?   They need to have the upward path of inquiry opened to them, hopefully, to be invited and stimulated to the search after truth !   Can we do nothing to kindle the glow of generous enthusiasm in their breasts—

the fire of an inextinguishable love of truth ? It
is not noble, in a professed philosopher to frown on
the spirit of inquiry, and to check and chill the effort
of speculative thought. It is not noble, to humble
and degrade the human mind, to exhibit its powerlessness, and to convict it of doing always and
only mischief. But in these Divinity lecture sermons, whatever be the subject, the heavy blow
comes down on man's intellectual powers. Whatever be the illustration, the lesson never varies—
how worthless, fallacious, and injurious are all
speculative efforts ! It is poor and pitiable work,
so to represent truth on the one hand, and the
mind of man on the other, as to leave no refuge
for a generous and high pulsing soul, absolutely
no refuge, but scepticism or despair.

I only add, on this section of the subject, that
there is a glaring inconsistency between the lecturer's views of the human mind in general, and
his own particular use of the instrument, when assailing rationalism. Beginning, from the outset,
with the position that the Infinite or Absolute is
wholly and only inconceivable, is not, in fact, an
object of human thought at all, he nevertheless
reasons on the subject with confidence, and with
an apparent total absence of effort. We are compelled to think, that at least *he* knows thoroughly
well. It is no difficulty, no labor to him. Like
an accomplished chess-player, he is so familiar

with the pieces and places, that he could make the moves blindfold, and check at every turn. The subject is not above him, but he is manifestly above it, and can handle it with perfect ease. The most impalpable distinctions he can pursue, the darkest processes of abstraction he can penetrate, and all the windings and ramifications of the highest ideas he can trace out. In this respect, the Bampton lecturer must not be confounded with Sir William Hamilton. Cousin,—after Helgel, and striving to bring the German schema some-what within the range of the common understand-ing, and to make it, instead of a pure ideal fig-ment, at least a little more consistent with the reality of things—had put forth, in brilliant capti-vating form, his Philosophy of the Infinite. This was a legitimate object of criticism. Hamilton simply criticizes it, takes the reasonings and posi-tions as given, brings them to the test of what he deems established principles, and concludes that the Infinite does not come within the legitimate sphere of philosophy, and is incogitable by the human mind. The Bampton lecturer, on the other hand, argues independently, constructs and spreads out his own processes of reasoning, as on a subject with which he was familiar, asserts confidently, and concludes decisively. Nevertheless, after all, he confesses, " I know actually nothing about the Infinite or Absolute, I can attach no idea to the words, they are perfectly, wholly, only inconceivable by my mind."

It is hardly a question, whether *this* does not vitiate the entire argumentation, to the very core, and from beginning to end. An impartial umpire might surely say, you reason as if you thoroughly understood your subject; and yet you assure me that you do not, that you cannot even conceive the ideas which you put into words. Which am I to believe, your course of reasoning, which is one thing, or your assurance, which is quite another thing? If you do not know, and cannot even conceive this Infinite or Absolute of which you speak, am I to think that you are nevertheless able to reason accurately concerning it; and am I to trust your reasonings, and to accept your conclusions? The *reductio ad absurdum* is a perfectly legitimate method, and quite satisfactory when fitly employed. But who ever heard of reducing to absurdity, a thing of which he was utterly ignorant, of which he could not even form the least conception? Are we not obliged to think that there must be some egregious fallacy, utterly fatal to the entire reasoning of this book on "the Limits of Religious Thought?"

SECTION THIRD.

CONCERNING A PHILOSOPHY OF "THE UNCONDITIONED," ETC.

CHAPTER I.

RELATION OF THE SCOTTISH AND OXONIAN PHILOSOPHIES.

Hamilton and Mr. Maurice—Scottish System—Chief Fault—Excellences—Entire Separation from Bampton Lecture—" The Unconditioned," etc.—Assumptions of Rationalism—Cousin—Realism of Hamilton—Wrote in Interest of Philosophy, and of Logic—Lecturer of Theology—Hamilton's Conclusions and his opposite.

THIS, perhaps, is the fitting place for attempting, presumptuous though it must seem, a brief vindication of the illustrious Scottish philosopher, with whom, and whose philosophy, the Bampton Lecture and its respected author, have been completely identified. First of all, for a moment or two, I may notice what, though in my humble judgment it be an entire mistake, is, I am sure, the farthest thing possible from a misrepresentation, on the part of Mr. Maurice, whose fervent, eloquent, and noble protest against the recently promulgated views of revelation, must deepen the already profound respect and love with which he is regarded. "Sir William Hamilton," says Mr. Maurice, "a logician in the most thorough and exclusive sense, was too consistent, and too honest, not to avow his

abhorrence of mathematics." (p. 156.)* "A brave
man doubtless, reckless of popularity, ready to
overthrow the discoveries of the generations past,
or the prospects of generations to come, rather than
sacrifice his consistency.   One cannot but honor
him for his sincere, cordial, unconditioned hatred
of that which had no meaning for him." (p. 156.)
No meaning for him!   I am not aware of the
ground on which this idea of Hamilton's utter
ignorance is based.   It seems to need something
like proof, and proof, I am convinced, would not
be easy to find.   But for his cordial and unconditioned hatred of mathematics, I must look upon
this, as an entire mistake.   He *does* indeed say
that the study of mathematics is not improving, in
the sense and in the degree in which its admirers
maintain that it is.   But he admits that *as a
mental discipline*, in which view, and in which
view alone, he speaks of it, "it is beneficial in the
correction of a certain vice, and in the formation
of a certain virtue.   The vice is the habit of mental
distraction ; the virtue is the habit of continued
attention." (p. 304.)† He, at the same time, quotes
with approval the words of no mean authority,
who asserts that the chief benefit of the study lay
"in strengthening the power of steady and conca-
tenated thought." (p. 305.)   Hamilton does say,
that the study is capable of leading to credulity on

* " What is Revelation," etc.   † " Discussions," etc.

the one hand, and to scepticism on the other hand. But the name which awakens so much reverence, Bacon, he brings forward as countenancing the same idea.

It ought not to be forgotten, that Sir W. Hamilton explains himself and his purpose, when he says, "we are far from meaning to disparage the mathematical genius, which invents new methods and formulas or new and felicitous applications of the old." (p. 285.) "Our objections and those of our authorities are directed against the *excessive* study of the mathematical sciences in general." (p. 321.) The case was simply this, as stated by himself—"the university of Cambridge, unless it can demonstrate that mathematical study is *the one best*, if not the exclusive, mean of a general evolution of our faculties, must be held to have established and maintained a scheme of discipline, more partial and inadequate than any other, which the history of education records." (p. 259.) "Some intelligent mathematicians," he adds, "admit all that has been urged against their science as *a principal discipline* of the mind, and only contend, that it ought not to be extruded from all place in a scheme of liberal education. With these we have no controversy." (p. 261) "The question," he says, "does not regard the value of mathematical science, considered in itself, or in its objective results, but the *utility* of mathematical study, that is, in its subjective effect, as an exercise of the mind. The expediency is not disputed of leaving mathematics, as a co-ordinate, to find their level, among the other branches of academical instruction. It is only contended, that they ought not to be made the principal, far less the exclusive object of academical encouragement." (p. 260.)

On the whole, perhaps it may be allowed, that this was, and still is, an open question, on which men may take the side taken by Hamilton, without either entire ignorance or cordial hatred of mathematical science, or its professors.

Whether I be right or wrong, in imagining any connection between this mistake and the supposed identification of Sir W. Hamilton with Mr. Mansell, so complete has the identification been, that in many quarters what praise or blame has been measured out to the one, has been supposed to be equally deserved by the other. In some cases, a prepossession in favor of the Scottish philosopher, in others a strong prejudice against him has been created ; both, I hope to show, alike unmerited. It is not forgotten by me, how much is justly due to the accomplished and learned author of the Bampton Lecture. I have not the power to injure his high reputation—I hope also, it is the farthest thing possible from my desire. Nevertheless, it will be maintained that he has misconstrued, and has totally misapplied and perverted Hamilton's doctrines.   Altogether, the design is to show, that the fundamental principles of the Bampton Lecture are very far apart indeed, from the principles, but especially from the genius and the spirit of the modern Scottish philosophy.

Sir W. Hamilton needs no eulogium from any one.   His labors and his writings are his monuments.   He belongs to Europe, and Europe, for ages to come, will cherish his memory and his work as among her rarest treasures.   Praise, from such as I am, would be simply presumptuous, with whatever genuine reverence and admiration I may look upon him.   But, it would be folly to claim for Hamilton's, or any other philosophical system, either faultlessness or perfection.   One flagrant error in it has often been singled out, it may be called, *the one* flagrant error, which more or less taints the whole.   It is the theory of causation, to which its author clung with intense, passionate fondness to the last, the impossibility of conceiving an absolute commencement (or an absolute termination) of finite phenomena.   But in spite of this great vice, the excellences of the system are many and grand.

1st.   The doctrine of external perception ; simple, profound, exhaustive, affording an impregnable philosophical basis for natural realism.   2d.   The doctrine of consciousness.   Kant had first completely revealed and interpreted this authoritative basis of philosophical induction. Cousin, also, had penetrated into its "arcana," with his subtle genius, and had irradiated them with the warm light of his fervid imagination. But to Hamilton we are indebted for the full analysis of the facts of consciousness, and for the rigid and logical exposition of its laws. 3d. The analysis and synthesis of the mental powers ; exact, complete, comprehensive ; are a lasting monument to Hamilton's fame. Even the mere nomenclature is an inheritance ; beautiful, suggestive, severely fitting. I. The acquisitive faculty—perception external and internal. II. The conservative faculty, memory proper. III. The reproductive faculty, recollection proper, under the laws of association. IV. The representative faculty, imagination. V. The elaborate faculty, the understanding. VI. The regulative or legislative faculty, reason.

I have said nothing of Hamilton's achievements in the sphere of logic, though competent judges declare them to constitute his highest triumph. But my information is too limited to authorize me to speak, and perhaps my power of appreciation is yet more limited still.

In comparing the modern English, and the modern Scottish philosophies, there is one feature of resemblance which it is impossible to deny. It is, here, acknowledged with great sorrow. The relativity of all our knowledge is maintained by Hamilton.

Entire and universal relativity is maintained, in the face, as we shall by-and-by strive to show, of considerations founded on experience, which go at least to modify the position. "Our whole knowledge of mind and matter is only relative, of existence absolutely and in itself we know nothing." (Lec. i. 138.) "All we know, is known only under the special condition of *our* faculties." (Lec. i. 140.) "However infinite and various may be the universe and its contents, these are known to us, not as they exist, but as our mind is capable of knowing them. Quicquid recipitur, recipitur ad modum recipientis." (Lec. i. 61.) "God only exists for us, as we have faculties of apprehending his existence." (Lec. i. 63.) Even so—thus far, the two *appear* to be in harmony. Perhaps it may come out eventually, that the harmony is more apparent than real, special rather than general. But to the points of contrast :—

I. The unvarying tone of the Bampton Lecture, we have seen, is repressive, humiliating and condemnatory of the efforts of the speculative understanding. But it is a fact, which hundreds at this moment would be eager to attest, that the living teaching of Hamilton was stimulative and quickening in the highest possible degree. If anything be certain it is this, that he inspired his students with an enthusiasm for speculative inquiry, a passion for investigation. And in this respect his writings are at one with his oral instructions. "Speculation," he says, "is not a negation of thought but the highest energy of the intellect." (Lect. i. 114.) The Bampton Lecture constantly exalts *faith*, in opposition to intelligence. Hamilton endorses the sentiment, that *doubt* is the first step to philosophy, and that the sceptical, searching, speculative spirit is indispensable in its disciples. Philosophy is the art of doubting well. (Lect. i. 90–93.) Again, supposing materialism to gain the ascendancy, he says, " Philosophy would then be subverted in the subversion of its three great objects, God, free-will and immortality"—the very three, from which especially and peremptorily, the Bampton Lecture would for ever shut us out; "true wisdom," he adds, " would then consist, not in speculation, but in repressing thought, during our brief transit from nothingness to nothingness." (Lect. i. 37.) We know where the repression of thought and the prohibition of speculation are demanded, with abundant plainness.

II. The entire separation of philosophy from theology, inasmuch as the latter belongs to the region of faith, is distinctive of the Bampton Lecture. Let us hear Hamilton's idea of philosophy, " It comprehends all the sublimest objects of our theoretical and moral interest : every (natural) conclusion concerning God, the soul, the present worth and future destiny of man is exclusively de-

ducted from the philosophy of mind." (Lect. i.
13.) "Mind rises to its highest dignity, when
viewed as the object, through which and through
which alone our unassisted reason can ascend to
the knowledge of God." (Lect. i. 35.) Need I say,
where we are taught that reason never can ascend
to this knowledge? Again, " the importance of
mental philosphy to theology has not become su-
perfluous in Christianity. Anterior to revelation,
religion rises out of psychology as a result, subsequently to revelation, it supposes a genuine philosophy of mind, as the condition of its truth."
(Lect. i. 42.) Again, after arguing on philosophical grounds for the priority of free intelligence in
the universe, he adds, "such is the manifest dependence of our theology on our psychology, in
reference to the *first* condition of a Deity—the absolute priority of free intelligence. But this is, perhaps, even more conspicuous, in relation to the
second, that the universe is governed not merely
by physical, but by moral laws, for God is only
God, insomuch as he is the moral governor of a
moral world." (Lect. i. 32.) " Thus it is shown,"
he says, " that theology is wholly dependent on
psychology, for with the proof of the moral nature
of man, stands or falls the proof of the existence
of a Deity." (Lect. i. 33.) If these passages fail
to mark a severance wide and fundamental I con-

fess myself unable to understand what like and un-like mean.

III. The last quotation suggests a characteristic of the Bampton Lecture, namely, the ethical principles maintained in it, which will fall to be examined at length in its proper place, and has not yet come before us. Here, it is taken forth only for a moment, and for the one purpose of contrast. No more unambiguous illustration of the contrast, perhaps, will be found, than is furnished by the perfectly opposite views taken of a passage in Kant's *Kritik of the Practical Reason.** It is that well-known, magnificent passage, beginning some-what thus:—" Two things, alike incomprehensible, lie clear before me, the starry heaven above and the moral law within ;" there follows a glorious and noble exposition of essential and immutable morality and of conscience as the revelation of it. Hamilton quotes it at length, with enthusiastic admiration as well of the soundness of the doctrine as of the stern sublimity of the expression. The Bampton lecturer simply ignores such a revelation of morality, and such authority in conscience. Is there no difference between the two ?

IV. Were everything else set aside, or satisfactorily explained, there remains one grand funda-mental doctrine, which places the two distin-guished men, of whom we speak, immeasurably far

---

* *Kritik der Practischer Vernunft,* s. 288. Riga, 1788.

apart from one another. It is the doctrine of the higher reason in man. Without the least hesitation, so far as concerns the work, on *The Limits of Religious Thought*, it can be asserted, that its author believes in no intellectual endowment, above the faculty of judgment, the understanding proper, the comparing and reasoning power. There may be occasional sentiments and phrases, that seem as if they pointed elsewhere, but throughout the distinct evidence is unvarying, abundant and decisive, that the highest of the mental powers is the mere understanding. But Hamilton places last and highest in his synthesis of intellectual endowments, reason, the *locus principiorum*, the place of native intuitions, of necessary, universal truths. He calls this, " the power which the mind has of being the native source of certain *à priori* cognitions." It is the regulative faculty, but not in the feeble sense of the Bampton Lecture, where regulative is used as equivalent to providing rules for practice and life. It is regulative, in the sense of regnant, legislative, insomuch as it gives forth laws of thought, creates mental forms, arising out of its own proper nature, according to which, knowledge and thought are moulded. It is not reasoning, and has nothing to do with reasoning, which, on the contrary, belongs wholly to the understanding, the lower reason. This reason does not reason, never can reason. Its only office is to

see what is written within, and to announce ac-
cordingly. It is the true *in-tel-lection*, though a
lower faculty commonly usurps this name. " The
human mind," says Leibnitz, " is not only capable
of *knowing* universal, necessary truths, but of *discovering* them in itself. There is a disposition, an
aptitude, a pre-formation, which determines our
mind *to elicit* these truths, and causes that they
can be elicited." So wrote the great German ;
and Hamilton, after reciting his words, adds, " I
have quoted these passages for their own great importance, as the first full and explict announcement, and certainly not the least able illustrations
of *one of the most momentous principles in philosophy*"—(Lect. ii. p. 359.) This principle, however, is entirely ignored in the Bampton Lecture.
It is not possible to exaggerate the extent and the
depth, the entirenss and absoluteness of the difference, arising out of the reception or rejection of
the doctrine of the higher reason, as the organ of
à priori truths.

I have done with the contrast ; and can now,
only in a single sentence, cluster together the points
which have been selected. 1st, in a spirit repressive of speculation and of philosophical inquiry,
and one stimulative and quickening in the highest
degree ; 2nd, in totally opposite views of the proper objects of philosophy and of the relation of
philosophy to theology ; 3rd, in no less opposite

views of conscience and of immutable morality ; and 4th, in a mere discursive understanding on the one hand and a higher reason on the other hand, the author of the Bampton Lecture is thoroughly and essentially separated from Sir William Hamilton. I am prepared to maintain, that wherever the philosophy of the able work, on the Limits of Religious Thought, may find its source, it is not and cannot be, in the system of Hamilton, the fundamental principles of which are utterly irreconcilable with its structure, its conclusions, and its entire tendency and spirit.

But the doctrine of " the Unconditioned, the Absolute, the Infinite" remains, and here, at all events, it may be conceived, it will be impossible to deny that the conclusions of these two distinguished men are entirely identical. I am very far, indeed, from being satisfied that this is at all the case.

We must look back to the account which was given in an earlier part of this criticism of German philosophical speculation ; of that account the use is, now, to be made, for which, chiefly, it was introduced. Be it then remembered, that Fichte, Schelling, and Hegel were not only metaphysicians and philosophers, but the acknowledged and admired leaders of metaphysical philosophy. Hegel, especially, was a profound logician and the master mind of his age. Nevertheless, we have seen, that the course of his speculation was, in many respects, consistent only with a thorough logical monomania. The same was nearly equally true of the others. Very frequently, the logical processes which they constructed might be rigidly sound. But one and all began in pure assumption, and throughout, necessitated, now and again, recourse to assumption. The Absolute of Schelling and Hegel and the absolute-*ego* of Fichte, at all events, the absolute of the two former was not only a mere *petitio principii*, but a mere abstraction. Being, Absolute being, in the naked, impoverished, most abstract sense of Hegel, was only the wildest figment of the logical intellect, and had no possible reality answering to it. And we have seen, in part, what conclusions, revolting to common sense, were built up out of this figment. Nevertheless, the mere dialectic freak of a powerful but, in this respect, uncontrolled understanding, was *the* theory of the universe, *the one* philosophy, at last discovered, *the* science of sciences. And it was hailed as such, over Germany, by the ablest and best men.

It was impossible that a man so intensely realistic as Hamilton, a believer in a real, external universe, a real individual soul of man, and a real God—all, with him, first principles of philosophy, immediate data of consciousness—could do anything but vehemently protest against this mania which, withal, had so much to captivate and allure a certain order of minds. Besides, himself as profound and . accomplished a logician as Hegel, how could he but indignantly spurn mere assumption and be shocked by daring, outrageous, even impious and, withal, baseless syllogisms? The German school of which we speak must by no means be confounded with the early sages of Greece and of Egypt. There is a profound and warm sympathy, which it is hardly possible to repress, when we listen to the wild rhapsodists of Elea, crying, as they did, amidst darkness and perplexity; or when we gaze on the ecstacies of Plotinus, Jamblichus, and Proclus: for they were men possessed and absorbed, surrendered disinterestedly, unreservedly, and wholly to what they passionately believed in. But we come in contact with quite another phase of experience, in the German school. I am far from denying the attribute of earnestness to Hegel, yet farther still from denying it to Schelling, and farthest of all from denying it to Fichte. But with Hegel, at all events, earnestness was a quality far more of the head than of the heart—it was intellectual, much more than either spiritual or moral. He had enthusiasm, an absorbing and overmastering enthusiasm, but it was the enthusiasm, not of religion, not even of philosophy, but almost purely of logic. He had a passion for subtlety, for system, and, whetted by success, it became a passion for victory, for scholastic supremacy. It seems to me impossible to resist the conclusion, that Hegel became, as it was quite natural he should, a bewitched and intoxicated lover of his own system—*the* system, as he and his disciples currently called it. All other realities were little to him in comparison with *the* system, *the* method. He sought to make them consistent with it, but he cared far more for it than for them. Invincible logic, all-conquering syllogism, were everything to him. That a whole nation, nearly, so far as its educated men were concerned, had caught this frenzy, had taken up, as the grandest reality, what rested on a mere assumption and worse, a mere abstraction, an idea, nothing real, not even possible, not even cogitable, was enough to vex and rouse a nature more phlegmatic than Hamilton's. But when, besides, it was attempted by Cousin to introduce *the* system to Europe, through a French medium, to modify, and soften, and rationalize it, surrounded with all the brilliance of a noble imagination and all the corruscations of a highly-cultivated genius, he could be silent no longer.

But—and attention is specially called to this fact—he wrote *in the interest of philosophy*. In the first instance, he wrote chiefly, if not solely, in the interest of philosophy, in the interest of the science of logic, whose legitimate sphere, he judged, had been wantonly abandoned. Logical formulæ and logical processes had been applied to certain abstractions—" The Unconditioned, the Absolute, the Infinite."   For philosophy's sake, he sought to demonstrate that a system of the universe, on such a basis, was impossible and absurd.   For logic's sake, he sought to demonstrate that these wild abstractions were not amenable to logical laws, were not compressible within logical forms, and were totally incognizable and incogitable.

The Bampton Lecture, quite on the other hand, is nominally, formally, altogether a theological treatise.   It is written *in the interest of Christianity*, and consists of " Divinity Lecture Sermons," according to the wording of the original foundation.   Its title is, *The Limits of Religious Thought Examined*.   The lecturer had nothing to do with philosophy, except indirectly ; nothing to do with the rationalism of Hegel ; nothing to do with these abstractions—The Unconditioned, the Absolute, the Infinite—unless they were to be held synonymous with the name of God, which neither Hegel, Cousin, nor Hamilton profess to maintain.   The distinction is fundamental.   Hamilton, in the first instance, at least, was discussing a question of pure metaphysics and of logic.

The lecturer was determining a religious doctrine.   But there is a second distinction.   It is not denied that Hamilton applied his philosophical conclusions to the more sacred sphere of theology, but such applications were partial and comparatively few. He holds and asserts, in the strongest terms, that *the* Unconditioned, *the* Infinite, *the* Absolute—these abstractions—are wholly and only inconceivable. But he never asserts, in the same way, that God is wholly inconceivable. I think we shall find that he asserts something very different, and totally opposite. *As Infinite*, he holds that God, *in his infinity*, is inconceivable, cannot be taken into thought. But this is all. Here are his very words: " The Divinity in a certain sense is revealed ;" could he have said *the* Infinite is, in a certain sense, revealed ? No : *the* Infinite, that ideal abstraction, that Pantheistic substance, is wholly inconceivable ; but with him *the Infinite* was not equivalent to God, but very much otherwise, for he says—" The Divinity is, in a certain sense, revealed ; in a certain sense, is concealed. He is at once known and unknown." Who can desire more than this ?

But the Bampton lecturer does not only not say this, but he says the very opposite. All the findings of Hamilton and his own, in reference to *the* Unconditioned, Absolute, or Infinite, he applies, without reserve or qualification, to the living God, as if they were the same. God, the true God, according to him, is wholly and only inconceivable by the human mind, " is not an object of human thought at all." Something is conceived ;

but it is not God, not God *as He is*, not very God; something is known, but it is not God. God, very God, is only and wholly unconceived and unknown. There are separate terms, occasional phrases, in the Bampton Lecture which seem to point to more than *this*. But taking, with the utmost stretch of candor, its deliberate reasonings, its express and repeated language, and its unvarying tendency and spirit, I think no impartial reader will deny that *this* is what it maintains.

7

CHAPTER II.

MEANING OF THE UNCONDITIONED, ETC.

" No Unconditioned," " No Absolute"—Never, to created Spirit—
"Infinite" Incomprehensible—Of, concerning, "Infinite"—No
Idea, then Nothing—Word Infinite understood—How ?—Infi-
nite not whole Sphere of Divine—Eternal—*This* Infinity proper—
All possible Attributes—Power, Knowledge—*He*, who Infinite,
not All-incomprehensible—Human Spirit and Highest—Human
Personality and Divine—Human Intelligence and Divine—Moral
Attributes and Divine—Man, true Microcosm.

THESE disastrous terms, the Unconditioned, the
Absolute, the Infinite ! How have they been im-
ported into theology, or even into philosophy ?
Above all, what authority is there for making
them convertible with the sacred word, God, the
name of the Only Living One, whom we have
been taught to call *our Father*, surely, not all unknown ?

Hamilton will tell us that " from Xenophanes
to Liebnitz, the infinite, the absolute, the unconditioned, formed the highest principle of speculation." This sentence, separated as it sometimes
has been by those who have quoted it, from what
immediately follows, not only may lose part of its
meaning, but may convey a totally different sense

from what is intended. Hamilton adds, "but from the dawn of philosophy in the school of Elea, until the rise of the Kantian philosophy, no serious attempt was made to investigate the nature and origin of the notion (or notions) as a psychological phenomenon." (*Discussions*, p. 18.) A certain ultimate point in speculation had been early reached, been thereafter assumed and pondered, but never deliberately and philosophically investigated, either during the Platonic, or the Alexandrian, or the scholastic periods, till the time of Kant and his immediate followers. Alexandrian philosophy, plunged in the mysteries of the "Logos," and rapt in ecstatic visions—the *vision* of pure being, a widely different thing from calm, patient *investigation*, had all but entirely passed this by. The marvellous dialectic subtlety of the schoolmen, save in a single instance or two, in the period of its highest excitement and energy, amidst the war of universals, and of sensible and intelligible species, dared not throw its weblike entanglement around their ultimate idea, dared not touch it. The silence and inaction of a thousand years are significant. Better, some will say, they had never been broken by the might and the mastery of Hegelianism. No, by no means. This highest principle, assumed so long, but never psychologically examined, lying dim and vague in the depths of certain philosophic minds, as a terrible secret which they *must* not question—this, philosophized and systematized, may reveal itself, as it never could have done, otherwise. Let us search to see.

Thought, it is said, in its farthest regress, its utmost effort to ascend to the ultimate, the highest, reaches a limit which it cannot transcend—absoluteness, unconditionedness. There must be something primitive, original, antecedent to all else, independent of all else. Be what it may, it must be absolute, unconditioned, infinite. Speculation asserts this, as its first principle, ponders it, goes forth after it, did so thousands of years ago. In the depths of eternity past, before the existence of a finite universe, there must have been absoluteness, unconditionedness, infinity, something absolute, unconditioned, infinite. That is the conclusion, or rather, the postulate. And it may here be allowed, that it is not unlawful to suffer thought to wander back, even though it can only weary itself in spasmodic efforts to transcend the limits of creation, and to conceive the Uncreated, alone, in immensity. Nor may this be wholly unconnected with an exalted, a rare veneration. But it is impossible not to feel, that this region cannot belong to *us*, save in a very exceptional sense. We *may* make the effort to pass into it, for a moment, but it can be but for a moment. Our moment's stay *may* awaken in our minds unusual sentiments of reverence and awe. We may meditate, and wait, and gaze, and be stronger and better for the effort. But the region, certainly, is not ours. We can KNOW nothing of it, however much we may conjecture; still less, can we reason confidently respecting it. It is the place, if place at all, not for reasoning, but for wonder and for abandonment to profound, uncontrolled emotion. When, therefore, it is reiterated from several quarters, *the* Absolute, *the* Unconditioned, *the* Infinite, *is, must be,* we can only ask, what do the words mean? Absoluteness, in the most wide and abstract sense, Unconditionedness, Infinity—certain qualities, attributes—but attaching to what, inhering in what? that is the question—a question to which we can obtain no answer. Is it something or nothing, or both, a being or a thing, living or dead, mind or matter? *The* absolute; it is a mere ideal figment, a thing of fancy, a pure self-imposition. There never was, or could be, a reality answering to such an abstraction.

It may be possible to imagine the non-existence of the finite universe, to conceive the Great Being, alone, in immensity; possible to conceive life, *then,* intelligence, *then,* one living intelligence. But when this is called *the* absolute, that is, absoluteness, in the abstract, who can attach a sense to the word? Absolute truth is quite intelligible. We understand by it, truth without mixture; very truth, and nothing **but** truth. And the Absolute

God would be intelligible ; meaning, very God, the real God, altogether divine, and alone divine. But this is not what is meant, but something perfectly different. It is the absolved God, God loosed from all relation, external and internal, *the* unconditioned, brought under no condition of relation or connection of any kind. One might answer, even so—let it be granted thus far, at least. The Great Being, before creation, alone, in immensity, must have been unconditioned, *ab extra ;* necessarily so, for there was nothing to condition Him. But what is gained ? This is only saying, that He was alone, in immensity, saying it in another form, without the slightest advantage. The statement *may* be true, at all events it cannot be denied. God was then, and must be conceived, as *the* unconditioned. But with that period and that state, save in mere abstracted contemplation, we have nothing to do ; and it is impossible, speculate as we may, that we can ever KNOW, certainly know, anything respecting it.

The era of creation, whenever, howsoever starting forth, the era of creation, *alone*, belongs to us ; and, in connection with this, I maintain that these terms—*the* unconditioned, *the* absolute (in the sense of absolved), not only have no meaning, but are thoroughly and utterly false. There is no being, or thing, in the universe to whom, or which they can apply. There is, there can be, no unconditioned God to us. The God of consciousness is not unconditioned. Consciousness never revealed, never could reveal, an unconditioned God. The mere fact of the existence of a conscious creature excludes the possibility of unconditionedness in the creator. The Great Being has voluntarily conditioned himself—that is, what we most certainly know—has voluntarily placed himself in relation with created beings and things. There is no such thing, evermore, as the unconditioned, the absolute ; if, indeed, there ever was such a thing. And how then shall we designate a philosophy, which, of its own proper motion, without cause given, brings up before us, and would perpetuate, these meaningless barbarities, which can only bewilder and darken ? How shall we designate the theology, which, through these monstrous fictions, raises an impassable barrier between the Almighty and his creatures, and, by the same means, strikes down the divinest thing in their nature, the reason He hath given them ?

The Bampton lecturer freely and constantly uses the phrase "*the* Absolute," as a name for the Deity, and *the Absolute* God, God in his *absolute* essence, *absolute* being. There is no absolute God, or essence, or being, in the sense of absolved, loosed from relation ; and if the word is employed, according to popular usage, to mean no more than true, real, very God, then the fault is not a small

one, of departing, in a philosophical work, from
the philosophical sense, and creating ambiguity
and error by a double meaning. Some, who are
far removed from the lecturer's standpoint, because the terms in question have come into such
prominence, not perceiving how injurious and how
false they are, have adopted them quite unhesitat-
ingly, as if they were true. The unconditioned,
the absolute, as phrases, occur very frequently,
without evil design, in our current literature and
theology. Perhaps, sufficiently valid reasons have
been produced to justify the demand, made in all
humility, but on ground which is deemed unassailable, that these barbarous, and most false words,
be banished from use for ever. They are meaningless, at the best ; there is no reality corresponding
to them. A true philosophy disowns them. A
true theology, still more.

But "*the* Infinite" remains, and, even in the
absence of the two cognate phrases, all the real
difficulty may yet abide unmitigated and entire,
compressed into the remaining term. Some objection might be taken to the form in which the
idea is put—*the* Infinite, that is Infinity, in the
abstract—where is it ? what is it ? I know of no
infinity but one. There is one Infinite Being.
Where else is infinity ? But God *is* Infinite ;
and the question rises up, as inevitably as if we
had still to deal with the terms, unconditioned

and absolute, is the Infinite conceivabie or inconceivable, cognizable or incognizable, by the human mind ?

On this point, I have to avow myself a humble disciple of Sir W. Hamilton, and so much the more, because I hold this to be perfectly consistent ; indeed, alone consistent with a thorough separation from the philosophy and the theology of the Bampton Lecture. To me, the reasoning of Hamilton is altogether invincible and invulnerable. It amounts to this, put in the simplest form—To think, is to condition, to limit, to bring within the conditions, the limits of our thinking power. That which has no limits, above, below, on this side or on that, cannot be placed within limits ; in other words, it *cannot* be thought. The Infinite is strictly unthinkable, because it is not limitable—limitable not in any exceptional sense, but in the true, literal sense of narrowing and circumscribing.

To think OF the Infinite, CONCERNING the Infinite, to form ideas, notions respecting it, is quite possible ; but to *think* it, that is, to *comprehend* it in thought, is strictly impossible. To think a thing in the strict, philosophical sense, that is, to bring it within thought, and to con-ceive it, or com-prehend it, amount virtually to the same thing. *Concipio, com-prehendo*, suggest an original, literal identity of meaning. To conceive, to form a concept of a thing exactly answering to the reality, to throw our thought around it and take it together, or again, to lay hold of it together, to close upon it with our grasp, are different forms of one substantial meaning, and that, again, is conveyed by the single word, *think*. To think a thing, is to grasp it within our thought. The Infinite cannot be grasped within our thought, nor within any limits, for, on all sides, it has no limits. To know God, *in his Infinity*, is impossible; but to know, and know much respecting *the* God, who is infinite, is quite another thing, and may be grandly possible. Meantime, I venture to suggest that the conclusion at which a sober philosophy arrives, is no other than that which men have already universally adopted, who know nothing of speculation or of metaphysical controversies. What they intend to convey, in saying that God is infinite, is, that they have thought and thought again and again, but have ever found the reality towering upward, piercing downward, stretching out on all sides immeasurably beyond their loftiest, farthest thoughts. Is it not so?

At the same time, there are some explanations to be put on this general conclusion, and some necessary reservations which have been often overlooked, and have thus occasioned great inaccuracy and even injustice, on the one side and the other. When, for example, it is broadly asserted that we can have no idea *of*, that is, *concerning*, the Infinite, the statement is at variance with facts, and with individual experience. Every one feels it, at once. That concerning which I have no idea at all, is to me nothing, in every sense, nothing. I may, and do believe in that which I cannot fully *com-pre-hend* in thought, which I cannot place clearly within my thought. But I must at least, be able to form some idea, some notion, as to what that is, which I cannot fully comprehend. I must so far have an idea concerning it, that I can distinguish it, from what it is not. To believe in that, respecting which I can form no notion, is to believe in nothing, it is not to believe at all. The nature which compels me to believe in the Infinite, must supply me somehow with a substratum, a substance of which my belief can take hold. Again, when it is broadly asserted that we can attach no meaning to the *word* infinite, this statement, also, is felt to be at variance with fact. We *do* attach a most distinct meaning to the word. Every one does, else how comes the word to be used. Historically, it stands simply thus : we have a certain notion or notions in our minds, and, in order to express them, we select, we create the word infinite, without limits, and are satisfied that this word is a proper and fitting medium for expressing what we mean. The word infinite, we understand perfectly : it means without limits ; but *the thing* which is infi-nite, we cannot com-pre-hend, con-ceive, think, bring into thought, and we simply mean to say that we cannot comprehend it, when we call it infinite. There is the word contradictory. We have a distinct and positive idea as to what we mean, when we say that a thing is contradictory ; but *the* thing which is contradictory, we cannot *think*, cannot take into thought, cannot conceive. Two and two are nine, it is a contradiction ; a piece of wood is two feet long and fifteen long, at the same time, it is a contradiction : it is *impossible to thought*. There is the word unintelligible. We know what it means ; but *the thing* which is unintelligible, we cannot *think*, cannot conceive, cannot comprehend. It is not *to be understood*. The very notion we have formed and expressed in the word, would be destroyed, if it were understood.

In the same way, we have quite a clear notion respecting what is meant by the word infinite, without limits. This is not difficult to our mind. We can reason respecting it ; we can apply it, and can judge when it is rightly applied, and when wrongly. But *that which is infinite*, we cannot con-ceive, and we mean to assert its inconceivability, when we say it is infinite. It is beyond thought, impossible to thought. Infinity, attach to what it may, where it may, is beyond thought, impossible to thought. Rightly, Hamilton suggests, that the word stands in human language as a symbol, not of the power, but of the powerlessness of the human mind ; not of knowledge, but of ignorance. And yet, is there not power as well as powerlessness ; is there not knowledge as well as ignorance betokened ; high, and stupendous knowledge. To know that Infinity belongs to the Great Being ; that in certain respects he is unknowable, lifted above the intelligence of his highest creatures : *this* is power, not weakness, this affects and elevates beyond measure our whole conception of Him. It is even this, which renders worship possible. But for this, there had been no God to us. A God all-known and comprehended, is no God. That which I fully know and understand is below, not above me, for I have mastered it. I have not to worship it, it must bow down to me. That which towers immeasurably above me, which I cannot scale and cannot fathom, before which I am as nothing, less than nothing, *that*, that alone, I fall down to and adore. Not ignorance, but knowledge, is the mother of devotion. Nevertheless, the sense of ignorance in the created mind, of immeasurable ignorance and inferiority, is preliminary and essential to all true adoration. " Who can by searching find out God, who can find out the Almighty to perfection ? It is as high as heaven, what canst thou know ? deeper than hades, what canst thou do ? the measure thereof is longer than the earth, and it is broader than the sea !"

But how do we come to predicate of any being

or thing this stupendous, incomprehensible attribute, Infinity, and in what sense is it predicable of
the one Great Being, and of Him alone ?   There
are sacred associations *here* not to be despised,
which do not surround either of the two mere
philosophical terms to which we before referred.
This word is hallowed to piety, because it is supposed to be sanctioned by the Holy Scriptures.
For the sake of those who might otherwise fail to
perceive how thoroughly open the whole question
is, I shall quote the only passages in Holy Scripture in which the term translated by our word infinite is found. They are four in number. " Ethio-
pia and Egypt were her strength, and it was infinite."   " Take the spoil of their infinite store."
" Are not thine iniquities infinite ?"   Only in one
instance is the word connected with the Almighty,
and that with reference to one of His attributes.
" Great is the Lord, His understanding is infinite."
Here, and in the other three examples, the word
simply means, without number, without search.
Not once, have we infinite, in the modern, philosophical and defined sense.

The Bampton lecturer, with Sir William Hamilton, maintains that the Infinite is given in consciousness, and given as the complement of our
consciousness of the finite.   Correlatives imply
one another.   It is not possible to think the one
without, in the same mental act, being necessitated

to think the other. Fully admitting the soundness of this logical law, there is, nevertheless, not much gained by it in the case before us. Logic and reality are by no means necessarily separated, but they are by no means necessarily connected. An idea shall suggest its correlate. In thought, both, shall be equally true, yet the one may have a positive reality answering to it, the other no reality at all. Something implies its correlate, not something, nothing. Being implies its correlate, non-being, Finite implies its correlate not finite, infinite. The one is a reality before me, the other, in two of the cases out of the three, is no reality at all, and whether, in the third it be a reality, *cannot*, at least only by such a method as this, be ascertained. Indeed, I am far from being satisfied that it is in this way at all, that we reach the notion of the Infinite.

That there is in the human soul a native, intuitive, original sense of God, of a Supreme Being, is one thing. But when Hamilton asserts that "*the* Infinite" is a datum of consciousness—asserts a universal conviction that the Infinite is—some hesitation is, perhaps, pardonable, for this is quite another thing. Two of the laws by which we test the data of consciousness are before me :—1st, the law of parcimony, namely, that no fact be assumed, except it be simple and ultimate ; 2nd, the law of harmony, namely, that nothing but the simple, ultimate fact be taken, without inference or addition. It appears to me that both of these laws are violated, when it is held that *the Infinite* is given in consciousness. In the educated, cultivated mind—the mind of a philosopher, a scholar —the datum may so grow into this form, that it shall not be judged susceptible of further analysis. But is there not an earlier, simpler form of the consciousness, truly the ultimate form, to which this makes an unjustifiable addition ? That there is a God is one of those *à priori* truths, those primitive cognitions, that lie in the depths of our higher reason, to which, in the words of Leibnitz, there is a disposition, an aptitude, a preformation, and which, though they may lie dormant, are ever capable of being elicited. There is a God, a Supreme, a highest Being, over all. But the datum is given in this grand, undefined form. That this Being is Infinite, I hold to be a conclusion of the understanding—a conclusion in certain cases so direct, immediate, and so strongly forced in upon us, as to be with difficulty distinguished from the original consciousness. Nevertheless, the two are perfectly distinct, and can be, and in strict truth ought to be, kept apart. The sense of God is universal, and native to the soul of man. But only this is universal. The conviction that the Supreme must be infinite is later, logically and chronologically, and is reached, however directly and rapidly, only through the understanding. But it *is* reached. There is no question here that the Great Being is infinite, truly and properly infinite is *the* Infinite One, the one only being of whom this attribute is predicable. Yet it is a question, a profound, even perilous question, one which demands investigation, and may also lead to great diversity of judgment—" In what sense and to what extent does Infinity belong to the Great Being ?"

The fallacy which pervades and vitiates the Bampton Lecture is, that this one attribute *constitutes* God, and since that which is Infinite is inconceivable, therefore He is only and wholly inconceivable, unknowable. No proof is attempted, but it is throughout constantly assumed that in all respects, and in every view, God is only *the* Infinite, and, therefore, the inconceivable.

There is one sphere in which, by consent of all, this stupendous attribute *must be* predicated. The *duration* of the Great Being is strictly *infinite*—unbeginning, unending, underived, uncaused, absolutely independent, unassailable, unchangeable, from everlasting to everlasting. How this conviction is reached, whether a direct datum of the higher reason, or a direct and irresistible inference from a datum of the reason, it is not here needful to inquire. There is no question to the philosophical theist, any more than to the Christian theo-

logian. But the con-cep-tion, the com-prehension,
to all is simply impossible. Take the image of a
perfect circle—without beginning, without end ; or
fancy a "*punctum stans ;*" or repeat the words
"an everlasting now"—no past, no future, no succession, no change, a perpetual present. But after
all these, or any such helps, we should count the
man bereft of reason who should profess that he
could in the most distant or feeble way approach
to the conception, the com-prehension, of eternal
duration. Here is Infinity strictly incognizable,
incogitable, in the sense in which those words have
been explained. But it is *believed*, and that supposes that we have formed some notion respecting
it, that we understand the words, and can see
clearly enough what *that* is which it is impossible
for us to com-pre-hend. It *is* believed. The lecturer holds it to be an immediate datum of consciousness. I may conceive it to be an inference
of the understanding from an original datum. But
in either case it is believed. That is the fact. And
is it nothing ? What creature on earth, except
man, is capable of reaching this truth at all—is
endowed with the faculty of believing it, of knowing that it is true ? This is no badge of weakness,
but much more a symbol of the greatness of our
nature ; that we *can* and do believe in One who is
unbeginning, unending, with whom is no succession, no change, but an everlasting present. A

majesty, a grandeur, an awfulness, are thrown around the Most High, which at the same time react on us. We are elevated, whilst we are over-awed. Our worship is not therefore ignorant, but only so much the more enlightened, because it is directed to One of whom we know that *that* is true, which is inconceivably above our highest thoughts.

The being or essence of the Supreme, inasmuch as it is unbeginning, unending, strictly eternal, must be infinite. The same is equally true of the attributes of the Supreme nature. *As eternal*, they are, each and all, strictly infinite. But explanation, elimination is attempted. The being of God is his proper nature, that whereby He is what He is, the *substans*, essence in which attributes inhere. When it is added, this essence is infinite *in itself* (and not merely in virtue of its eternal duration), I, for one, am unable either to affirm or deny. I can attach no sense whatever to the words. It may be great ignorance, great obtuseness, great incapacity. But I can form no sort of notion, what *that* is which is maintained. It may be true, or it may be false, but I am quite incapable of understanding the one or the other. Logic would make short and decisive work of this difficulty, if it be a difficulty. The Divine essence, we should be told, must be either finite or infinite ; if it be not finite, then it must be infinite. Yet this also admits of an answer, short, if not decisive. Who shall determine for us that these words, finite and infinite, are at all applicable in this case? I think they are not. Heat is neither long nor short. Light is neither round nor square. These qualities have no relation to the substances named. Were it asserted that the Divine essence is limited, finite, the ready questions would start up, how, where, in what sense? It is impossible. There is, there can be nothing to limit it. This is *the one* essence in the universe, the being of beings, the primitive nature, *the one* fountain of all other natures. Whence could a limit arise? It is contradictory —would be destructive.

But, infinite *in itself!* I can attach no meaning whatever, to the language. In my humble judgment, to be incapable of limit and to be infinite are not the same, but totally different. When the duration of the Great Being is declared to be un-beginning, unending, there is certainly *a positive idea* conveyed, though we be unable to grasp it in our thought. It is more, much more, than being incapable of being limited, it is something positive and actual in itself. And it is this which I, for one, am unable to attach any meaning to, in con-nection with the Highest essence, the Highest na-ture. Incapable of being limited is one thing, posi-tive Infinity, as in the case of duration, is quite another thing. Loosely, expletively, rhetorically, we speak of the Infinite Life, the Infinite Essence, without harm, possibly even so as to awaken reverent feeling. But, beyond this, if with the view of exalting the Almighty, men have attributed positive *infinity* to his nature, *in itself*, they have done so, on their own authority. Men have originated this application of a sacred word; a man may question its propriety and its truth.

Pursuing still this special course of thought it is farther maintained that, when it is said that the Supreme Being is enriched with all possible attributes to which not one in any direction can be added, this is the utmost that can be said. To talk of an infinity of attributes is to utter not only what has no meaning, but what is contradictory, landing us in the absurdity of an infinite number. And, *in like manner*, the application of the term infinite to the separate excellences (except in virtue of their eternity) of the Most High, may be shown to be not only unmeaning but false. For illustration, I select two Divine properties, which seem to afford the most appreciable example of what I seek to convey—power and knowledge. Shall we say, Infinite power, Infinite knowledge? With genuine desire to honor their Maker, men have uttered these expressions; but they rest solely on human authority. What do we really mean when we so speak? The infinite God, He who is strictly, properly infinite, knows all the knowable and can effect all the powerable. Is not this what we mean, and all that we mean? But that all the powerable and all the knowable amount, each, to infinity who can determine? None can. There is no limit to the power of the Highest; all that belongs to the sphere of power is His. There is no limit to the knowledge of the Highest; all that belongs to the sphere of knowledge is His.

It comes to this. The God revealed in consciousness is the Highest Being, beyond whom nothing is possible. The understanding infers that his duration must be unbeginning, unending, strictly infinite; infers besides, that every possible attribute, physical, intellectual, and moral, in the highest possible degree, must inhere in his nature. On every side, in relation to every quality, the Supreme must tower immeasurably beyond the highest conceptions of his highest creatures. The understanding concludes that he does, and adores Him, *Him alone*, as God. There is a sense in which the Highest is thus for ever unknown and unknowable. But this conclusion of the understanding, in its very nature and in the very mode in which it is reached, involves that there is also a sense, in which He is truly known and for ever to be more and more known. Infinity is all-incomprehensible, but infinity does not extend,—*cannot*, in the nature of things—extend over the whole sphere of the Divine. The Being who is truly infinite, is not *all*-incomprehensible. Wherein and how far is he comprehensible?

That is the question to which we now address ourselves.

Sir William Hamilton, whom the Bampton lecturer professes to follow, shall here be our guide, and shall show us the pathway to this highest knowledge. "Though man," he says, "be not identical with the Deity, still he is created in the image of God. It is, indeed, only through an analogy of the human with the Divine nature, that we are percipient and recipent of the Divinity." (*Discussions*, p. 19.) And in these memorable words: "Mind is the object, the only object, through which our unassisted reason can ascend to the knowledge of God." From mind, from the spiritual nature within us, according to Hamilton, we rise, legitimately rise, to the spiritual nature above us and over all. Merely, *as essence*, as *substans*, we are utterly ignorant of our own minds. But the man would be unworthy to be reasoned with, who should, therefore, deny that we had any *real* true knowledge of them. A mental image of spirit, as distinguished from matter, we certainly have not, for to that all materials are wanting. But we have a clear, fixed idea of a spirit dwelling within us, the residence of spiritual attributes and the source of spiritual life and energies. From our own, we rise, legitimately rise, to the uncreated, all-creating Spirit, and *can* and do conceive—never adequately, never with full comprehension, but in a way which satisfies, while it overawes reason and awakens the profoundest veneration—*can* and do form a conception of Him who is the fountain of all spiritual being and excellence. This is the first step in that mystic ladder, whereby, according to Hamilton, our unassisted reason *can* ascend to God. The second is no less direct.

From our own personality and individuality, we rise to the conception of One Supreme Being. The logical enigma of the One and the Many, the One and the All, of which Mr. Mansell makes so much, creates little perplexity in actual experience, save in rare instances. I do not, dare not, make light of it. Too well I know, how it has crushed and tortured many an earnest soul, from the day when the burdened singer of Elea sent up his wail, till now. But as a matter of fact, men have learned, save in rare instances, to argue very simply, but very soundly. We are one, yet have many powers. How our unity is not destroyed by this plurality we cannot explain, but we certainly know the fact that *it is not* destroyed. How the I, that thinks, and feels, and acts, is not a bundle of thoughts, and emotions, and acts, but separate, independent, beneath and above them all, we cannot explain ; but we certainly know the fact, and accept it, and act upon it every hour, and find it perfectly intelligible. The logical dilemma is not, save in rare instances, either an intellectual or a moral difficulty. Our separate unity and individuality, and our entire identity at all stages of our being, are, according to Hamilton, and, we presume, Mansell also, original data of consciousness. And the unity and individuality of the Great Supreme present no difficulties which have not been met and practically surmounted in the case of our own personality. So we plant our foot firmly on the second step of the ladder which connects legitimately, truly connects the human with the Divine.

A third and a fourth step are close at hand. From intelligence within we rise to intelligence above us; from moral attributes within we rise to supreme moral excellence above us. In these two last respects, the principles of the Bampton Lecture, as to the inconceivability of the idea of God, are in directest contradiction to the ordinary convictions of men. We *certainly* know what an intelligent, what a moral nature means. The intelligence and moral perfection of the Supreme may be immeasurably beyond our highest conceptions. But knowledge and rectitude, and purity, and love are real qualities, independent of quantity. Wisdom is wisdom, rectitude is rectitude, love is love, whatever be the sphere over which they extend. Wisdom on which no limit can be put, I cannot comprehend in my thought. But what wisdom is, I clearly understand, and am able to form a higher and still higher idea of its extent; and if still far above my highest idea, it stretches out, *it* is all the while distinctly in my thought, though to its full sweep I cannot reach. Infinity is for ever beyond the grasp of my conceptive faculty, but wisdom is not, moral attributes are not ; and a spiritual nature, in which wisdom and moral attributes dwell, is not. Even to say that the attributes, intellectual or moral, are of an extent which I can never fully comprehend, makes only a new and grand addition to my idea of the nature in which they dwell ; instead of destroying my conception, this makes it only more real and more lofty.

Man is thus the true microcosm. His material frame allies him with the visible universe ; his rational nature allies him with the invisible Creator of the Universe. It is not faith, but scepticism, which proclaims it impossible for reason to ascend to the conception of God ; a scepticism, which is in the face of our deepest convictions and of the facts of experience ; a scepticism, we shall find, which, having first laid the chief attribute of humanity in the dust, proceeds to strip revelation of all its glory, and to make it not an unveiling, but a concealing of the Most High—an elaborate and distressing disappointment.

SECTION FOURTH.

CONCERNING WRITTEN REVELATION.

———•———

CHAPTER I.

Must believe God is—That Intelligent—Free Intelligence—Benignant, Truthful—These Conclusions Indispensable—If not reach, no Revelation to Man.

It was not to be demanded that the Bampton lecturer should enter into any formal proof of the divine authority of the Old and New Testaments. He has not done so. It was by no means necessary in relation to his special subject. We shall grant, that supposing a revelation at all, he was entitled to assume *the* actual revelation in the Holy Scriptures. But what of the preliminary question of a revelation at all? This had a connection, a very close and startling connection with his subject. So much so, that at this moment it is to me unaccountable, almost incredible, that he could have overlooked it. Without reasoning at all, let me put the case as it may be supposed to strike any ordinary understanding. "Here is a revelation from God." "From God? one asks, who has yielded to the previous reasonings of the book. From whom, did you say?—God? Who is He? where is He? what is He? You have proved to me that my understanding is incapable of guiding me to know anything about God, and that I can never, through my understanding, know anything certainly about him. You have proved to me, that I can never come to a fixed conclusion for myself, that there is a God. You have proved to me that, in the absence of written revelation, a rational Theism is absolutely impossible ; that all thought, and all speculative reasoning on the subject, can only land me in insoluble contradictions and absurdities. Do not mock me ; do not add insult to injury. A revelation from God ? I must first of all know that there is a God, and you have told me that *this* I cannot know. I must first of all know something about God ; aye much, very much, about him ; much that is important and essential, before I can even look at what calls itself a revelation from Him."

Perhaps it would have been more exact, to say that the lecturer has, *in effect* overlooked the facts which I have expressed in this imaginary reply. *In words*, he has acknowledged them ; but the words are few and loose. The acknowledgment is made as if little or nothing depended on it, and as if the facts were of little or no importance, and presented no difficulty in relation to the general argument. The entire passage runs thus :—" But before applying this method to the peculiar doctrines of the Christian revelation, it will be desirable to say a few words on the preliminary condition, on which our belief in the possibility of any revelation at all is dependent. We must justify, in the first instance, the limitations which have been assigned to human reason in relation to the great foundation of all religious belief whatsoever ; we must show how far the same method warrants the assertion which has already been made on other grounds, namely, that we may and ought to believe in the existence of a God, whose nature we are unable to comprehend, that we are bound to believe that God exists, and to acknowledge him as our Sustainer and our Moral Governor, though we are wholly unable to declare what he is in his absolute essence." (pp. 170, 171.)

In this quotation, the phrase, Moral Governor, occurs, though where the writer finds it, it is hard to see. He does not tell us, nor what sort of connection he supposes it to have with the acceptance of revelation. The idea is not taken up at all, either here or elsewhere. Even the phrase is not introduced again. All that is in any way looked at by the lecturer, in the passage now quoted, is that we must believe that God exists, though He be wholly and only inconceivable by our minds. This belief in God, which lies at the foundation of theology, he then, at some length, places by the side of the belief in causality, which lies at the foundation of philosophy. Theology, it is made out, is not worse than philosophy. The one rests on what it cannot conceive, so does the other. That is enough. Were it at all of importance, it might be possible, with great ease, to resist this parallel. Philosophy asserts that for every event, there must be cause. But do we not distinctly know what we mean, by the word cause ? We certainly do. How the notion of cause originates, whether *à priori* or *à posteriori*, or partly both, is a question which has long been agitated, and may yet be unsettled. It is even keenly discussed, whether there be such a thing as causality at all, and whether all phenomena may not be resolved into mere succession in time, or place, or both. But what is meant, when we speak of that which is properly cause, is no question, never has been a question. Power expresses the causal nexus, with abundant distinctness and is perfectly conceivable. Why power should be necessary, why for every event we should be compelled to believe a cause we know not, and can assign no reason. But that is all. On the theological side, on the contrary, why there should be a God, why we are necessitated to believe in a God, is not the point which troubles any mind. The lecturer does not say it is, but something perfectly different. He maintains that the very idea of God, at all, we cannot conceive, and that we know and understand nothing about him ; *except that He is.* Even so.

But this is literally all that is advanced, on what is admitted to be a " preliminary condition on which our belief in the possibility of any revelation at all is dependent." " We are bound to believe that God exists," says the Lecturer. And what, then, of the contradictions, theistic, pantheistic, atheistic, into which we are inevitably plunged, so soon as we dare to think ? Are they to be all forgotten ? Must we not first of all get rid of them ? But how ? *Who, what* shall extricate us from them ? Unless from within, extrication is impossible. But let this pass. God is given in consciousness, the lecturer will say. Let it be granted. But through what power of our nature do we take hold of this ultimate fact ? Consciousness is a general term, which applies equally to all our acts of knowledge, all our feelings, and all our convictions. Somehow or other, that which we distinguish as reason in man, the higher reason, our unassisted reason, *must* be able to ascend to God, in spite of all the alleged contradictions. There must be no talk of building up a consciousness, of constructing a notion. *This* is original and universal, or it is not. If it be not, then away with that necessity of belief, which the lecturer admits and enforces. If it be, let us neither add to it, nor take from it. This is an intuition of our nature—the lecturer admits it, Hamilton contends for it—a primitive, native, *à priori* cognition ; and its place can only be, the higher reason.

There is an organ—it appears—a special power in our mental constitution, through which we ascend to the highest. From that inner sanctuary of our being, there comes forth the voice, " There is a God, a Supreme over all." " We must believe in God." But in what ? something or nothing ? To say that we believe in God and yet that we have no idea of Him, is neither more nor less than a direct contradiction.

The pathway by which unassisted reason *can* ascend upward, I have already, under the guidance of Hamilton, sought to describe. From ourselves, we rise to the Highest. Infinity it is impossible ever to compass in thought, but He who is truly Infinite, we can and do conceive of, and in our measure, know. Every son of man in whom is the sense of the Great Being, has also, by the same token, formed his idea of that Being, more or less imperfect, but also more or less true and real. Here, then, is the first necessary preliminary condition of belief in any revelation. On some independent ground, through some power of our nature, we must *beforehand* have reached the conviction that there is a God.

2d. Not less essential is the condition, that we be satisfied that this God is endowed with intelligence. A message from Him ! Are we satisfied that He can instruct us, that He can have anything great and worthy to communicate? Unless we be, it is impossible for us even to admit the idea of a message from Him at all.

3d. A God under the law of universal necessity, subject to a force over which he has no control, is not one who could communicate with his creatures. He must be governed by his own free choice, and have the power of adopting measures, arising out of the condition of those in whom He is interested, and out of the purposes of his own intelligence. Only a free being can be conceived to reveal himself.

4th. The conviction is indispensable of the perfect truthfulness of the Supreme. I might have added, his good will; for who could open the message of a possibly malignant Deity. But at least perfect truthfulness is absolutely essential. The lurking idea of falsehood, the faintest suspicion of deception, would be utterly fatal to any communication between the Creator and his creatures.

Thus, then, it stands. *That reason*, which Mr. Mansell represents as so feeble and so false, *must* have real power and of no inconsiderable amount. If *he* cannot trust it, at least the Great Being puts confidence in it, and commits to it some high and hard questions and some most momentous interests. If *he* can find nothing but darkness in its path, nothing but contradictions and absurdities as its results and no destiny for it for ever, but hopeless wandering amidst the dreary mazes of Pantheism and Atheism, the Great Being must have far different thoughts, for He entrusts it, it alone, with the determination of preliminaries, all but infinitely important. Somehow or other, before even looking into what professes to be a revelation, our minds, for themselves, *must have* been able to reach the conviction, not only that there is a God, but that He is an intelligent, a voluntary, a moral—at least in the sense of truthful—being. We cannot go to the revelation for proof of one of these things. Unless they are all sure beforehand, we cannot, as rational beings, must not, dare not open it at all.

Imagine the Bampton lecturer, requiring only belief in a God of whom we can form no conception, presenting the volume of revelation, strong in the outward tokens of its origin, to the rationalist with whom he has been reasoning. With what bitterness, what desolation of heart, would he answer: " You have put out my eyes, and do you call on me to behold the daylight ; you have destroyed my organ of hearing, and do you tell me there are words of melody to which I should listen. Your external proofs are excellent, no doubt, and satisfactory to those who can understand them. But you have assured me that ' my mind is a perfect blank,' in reference to the essential nature of

God, and that I have no means of knowing, in any one direction, *what* He truly is. Perhaps he is destitute of intelligence, and this book could only lead me into error and folly. Perhaps it is the work of an invincible necessity, and I have not even the satisfaction of knowing that it is what *He* wishes to communicate. Perhaps He hates me, at all events has no regard to truth, and this book may be a tissue of malignant untruths."

There is no answer but one to all this—the fundamental principles of the Bampton Lecture must be unsound. Were they true, revelation would be impossible. We could never come in contact with it. We should want the indispensable preliminary means for coming into contact with it. I deliberately maintain, that were the principles of the Bampton Lecture true, not a single son of man could reach those conclusions, which are indispensable, before he could rationally open the pages of a professed revelation. But they are not true. Every enlightened believer in revelation is a witness against them. Our minds are not perfectly blank, as the lecturer asserts they are, in reference to the essential nature of the Great Being. They can and do reach, they are constituted to reach the conception of a Supreme, Intelligent, Voluntary, Moral Nature. Formed by the Almighty, it is not strange that they should, it would be passing strange if they could not. "Mind is the object,

the only object"—I do not promise that this shall
be the last time I shall fortify myself in this criticism by referring to these compendious and memorable words of Hamilton—" through which our unassisted reason can ascend to the knowledge of
God."

CHAPTER II.

External Evidence—What?—Impossible to Multitudes—In Full-
ness to Any—Book, Divine in Origin—Contents Unknown—
Faith to Seek—Internal Evidence—What?—Self-attestation—
Its Power.

THERE are obviously two methods, one or other,
or both of which might be adopted in dealing with
what claims to be a message from heaven. Either
it might be asked, if its *contents* be such, so true,
so pure, so great, so new, and otherwise unknown,
so consistent with all that had before been reached
respecting the character of the Great Being, as to
show beyond doubt whence it comes. Or it might
be asked, if the outward tokens and seals of its
origin be such, as not only to put down all suspicion, but to create entire conviction. The Bampton lecturer allows, in some sense, the propriety of
both of these methods, but he expresses very clearly
his distrust, almost dislike of the first, and his
strong preference of the second. "The reasonable
believer must abstain from pronouncing judgment
on *the nature* of the message, until he has fairly
examined the *credentials* of the messenger." (p.

169.) " If there is sufficient evidence on other
grounds, to show that the scripture in which this
doctrine"—one that is perplexing and dark—" is
contained, is a revelation from God, the doctrine
itself must be *unconditionally received*, not as reasonable nor as unreasonable, but as scriptural.   If
there is not such evidence, the doctrine itself will
lack its proper support, but the reason which rejects it is utterly incompetent to substitute any
other representation in its place." (p. 180.)   " We
are thus compelled to seek another field for the
right use of reason, in religious questions"—*i. e.*,
than by examining doctrines and judging of their
consistency and truth—" and what that field is, it
will not be difficult to determine . . . . in
other words, the legitimate object of a rational
criticism of revealed religion is *not* to be found in
the *contents* of that religion, but in its *evidences*."
(p. 234.)   " The crying evil of the present day in
religious controversy is the neglect or contempt of
the external evidences of Christianity : the first
step towards the establishment of a sound religious
philosophy, must consist in the restoration of those
evidences to their true place in the theological system." (p. 238.)   " We do not *certainly know* the
exact nature and operation of the moral attributes
of God. We can but *infer* and *conjecture* from
what we know of the moral attributes of man, and
the analogy between the finite and the infinite can

never be so perfect, as to preclude all possibility of error in the process." (p. 240.) "The evidence derived from the internal character of a religion, whatever may be its value within its proper limits, is, as regards the divine origin of the religion, purely negative. It *may* prove in certain cases (though even here the argument requires much caution in its employment) that a religion has *not* come from God, but it is *in no case* sufficient to prove that it has come from Him." (p. 238.) "Even the negative argument, which concludes from the character of the contents of a religion, that it cannot have come from God, however legitimate within its proper limits, is one which requires considerable caution in the application." (p. 239.)

On the whole, it is quite indisputable, that the Bampton lecturer looks to the external evidences of revelation, as alone positive and reliable. The internal evidence is at best negative, and always doubtful. In these circumstances, it is of no small importance to ascertain what are those external evidences, on which almost everything, indeed, in effect *everything* depends, in order to a rational faith, in divine revelation. We again quote the lecturer's own words :—"Here then is the issue which the wavering disciple is bound seriously to consider. Taking into account the various questions, whose answers on the one side and the other, form the sum total of evidences for or against the claims of the Christian faith ; the genuineness and authenticity of the documents, the judgment and good faith of the writers ; the testimony to the actual occurrence of prophecies and miracles, and their relation to the religious teaching with which they are connected ; the character of the Teacher himself, that one portrait, which in its perfect purity and holiness, and beauty, stands alone and unapproached in human history, or human fiction ; those rites and cermonies of the elder law, so significant as typical of Christ, so strange and meaningless without Him ; those predictions of the promised Messiah, whose obvious meaning is rendered still more manifest, by the futile ingenuity which strives to pervert them ; the history of the rise and progress of Christianity, and its comparison with that of other religions : the ability or inability of human means to bring about the results, which it actually accomplished ; its antagonism to the current ideas of the age and country of its origin ; its effects as a system on the moral and social condition of subsequent generations of mankind ; its fitness to satisfy the wants, and console the sufferings of human nature ; the character of those by whom it was first promulgated and received ; the sufferings which attested the sincerity of their convictions ; the comparative trustworthiness of ancient testimony and modern conjecture ; the mutual contradictions of conflicting theories of unbelief and the inadequacy of all of them, to explain the facts, for which they are bound to account ;—taking all these, and SIMILAR *questions* into *full* consideration, are you prepared to affirm, as the result of the whole inquiry, that Jesus of Nazareth was an impostor, or an enthusiast, or a mythical figment, and his disciples crafty and designing, or well-meaning, but deluded men ? For, *be assured*, that nothing short of this, is the conclusion which you *must* maintain, if you reject *one jot or one title* of the whole doctrine of Christ." (pp. 248-9.)

This is the course, and by no means *the whole* course, through which men immersed in the business of daily life, unused to continuous study, incapable of it, through which the unlearned, unprivileged, ignorant multitudes must pass before they can get to a rational, satisfactory faith in Christianity ! *Credat Judæus !* There must be some grand mistake here !

The closing sentence in the quotation just made, does not much lie in our way, but it is too singular to be passed without notice. Surely this is not dignified ; it sounds like an argument *ad terrorem*, which most ingenuous and honorable minds would be tempted to resent. *Be assured*, nothing short of this is the conclusion, which you *must* maintain, if you reject *one jot or one tittle* of the whole doctrine of Christ." Either the Bible, as it is received at this day, entire, or inevitable scepticism. If this be not the meaning, what else can it mean ? But is it true ? Is the warning, the intimidation, well grounded ? Is the alternative actually what is here stated to be ? Some good Christians are often perplexed by the conflicting genealogies in Matthew and Luke, and especially because both alike refer not to Mary, but to Joseph. Others are troubled respecting the authority of the Gospel, which bears Matthew's name. It is well known, that Luther rejected the epistle of James from the canon. Many do not accept the epistle to the Hebrews, and still more are in doubt respecting the Book of Revelation. I am not called upon to say yea or nay to these and other such subjects of dispute. But I accept the fact. They are points in dispute among faithful Christians, and surely they are not beyond the sphere of legitimate criticism. The Bampton lecturer has too summary a method of dealing with them all, as if he were ready to put in practice a universal ostracism. "*Be assured* there is no alternative, if you reject one jot or one tittle of the whole doctrine of Christ." There is something not pleasing in this spirit, which more than once betrays itself in the book on the limits of religious thought. It would be wrong to assert that this was the conscious design of the author ; but ever and again the words of the book seem framed to bewilder, and terrify, and drive per force into faith.

After the long array of external evidences in the passage just quoted, it is added:—"taking all these *and similar* questions into full consideration, &c." Ample as the enumerations had been, it is quite true, that there *are* similar questions, an almost endless number of similar questions, which demand an answer, quite as imperatively as those that are specified, before a result satisfactory to the understanding can be obtained. I can jot down but a few headings—Ancient Documents, their age, transmission, purity, authority; Ancient History, Egyptian, Arabian, Persian, Chaldean, Hebrew, Grecian, Roman; Chronology, Geography, Natural History, Astronomy, Geology—then, Philology, Criticism, Principles of interpretation; Inspiration, its meaning, its evidences, its degrees, how claimed by the writers, how far allowed by antiquity; the Canon, by whom determined, When, by What authority.

The field is almost illimitable, and be it remembered, if the demands of the understanding are to be satisfied, it must be *all* overtaken. Not one thing, in such a case, can rationally be assumed on authority. If one thing may, another may, *all* may be assumed, and the whole ground is shifted and destroyed. If the basis of faith is to be an examination of external evidences a process of calculation and computation, a work of the logical understanding, then it must be complete and exhaustive if it is to be rationally available. A single decided flaw, a palpable gross blunder in history, chronology, or science, in a quarter which we had not looked into, would be sufficient to overturn any structure we had previously reared. The mind could have no rest, so long as a single region of evidence had not been thoroughly explored.

Far, very far, am I from denying that it is wise and dutiful, not only for professional, but for non-professional persons, to investigate, as they have opportunity, one or other, or more of the branches that are included in the external evidences of revelation. The result of such investigation, rightly conducted, will be to confirm faith, and to create profound wonder at the minuteness, the nice adjustments, the continuity and the strength of the proofs. The result will be to awaken the feeling that further study, in other and new directions, could only end in the same confirmation of faith, and the same strengthening wonder. But no intelligent man could fail to perceive, that when only a small portion of a field almost unlimited had been visited, and when a single fact, in any one of the unvisited regions of that field, might be sufficient to change the whole face of things, he could have—were this the kind of basis on which his faith must rest—no rational peace till every spot and corner had been thoroughly explored.

Far, very far, am I from undervaluing the learned, impartial, indefatigable workers in the manifold departments of the external evidences. Revelation has everything to hope for from them. The world, the church lies under an amount of obligation to them, not easily estimated. The antiquarian, the scientific, the hermeneutical, especially the historical, the philological, and the critical branches of sacred learning, are of incalculable value, and have amply repaid the talent, the research, and the time that have been devoted to them. They *must not* be forsaken, they *cannot* be spared, and, happily, there is little token that labor in this direction is likely to flag. Far otherwise. But I speak to the nature of things. If no single lifetime, devoted only to this, could overtake all, or nearly all, that is included in the external evidences of revelation, and if unless *all* be overtaken, there can be no legitimate rest to the understanding, in this species of proof, is it conceivable, is it possible, that the Most High should send a message to his creatures, which could be satisfactorily authenticated in no other way than this? It is impossible. It is contrary to all reason, to all probability. One might venture to affirm, without exaggeration, that if rational faith be of the nature supposed, there is not a rational believer in revelation, in existence, at this moment. There never has been a rational believer in revelation, not one individual, in any age, who has so thoroughly, so exhaustively gone over the whole of the external proofs, as to be able to say with truth, " There is not a corner, which I have not explored, not a spot, in which some seemingly decisive fact against the authority of Scripture might lie, which I have not narrowly scanned. The thing is literally, physically impossible.

It is no calumny against professional men, to say that few of them either have, or can have exhaustively searched into more than one or two of the leading and better-known branches of external evidence. Many, very many, have not, cannot have done even this. What, then, of non-professional persons, of the vast laity, especially the vast commonalty of Christianity ? Talk of Hebrew, Greek, Chaldaic, Syriac, and other languages of ancient codices, ancient versions, of historical, scientific, philological, critical, hermeneutical researches and studies, of prophecies and miracles and inspiration, and the kinds of investigation belonging to them ! What do, what can, the myriads of good Christian people know about any of these things ? Nothing, absolutely nothing. And have they, then, no positive, reliable evidence, on which their faith rests ? Has the Great Being left them without *the possibility* of any positive, reliable evidence ? For in their case, such faith, as Mr. Mansell desiderates, is literally, absolutely impossible. With patent, outcrying, innumerable facts around us, we cannot hesitate to judge that the Bampton lecturer must be wrong, altogether wrong, in this conclusion. The evidence which alone he counts positive and reliable is that which untold myriads cannot reach *by any possibility.* The evidence which he counts merely negative, is that on which their faith rests, on which it must rest, for they have no other. The question gives its own reply—a triumphant reply. Must not *this* evidence, *and not the other,* be the highest, the soundest, the strongest? It would be an impeachment of the Almighty to think anything else, it would betray, on his part, a manifest disregard of the pressing wants and the dearest interests of his creatures.

There is more. On the face of it, external evidence can bring only to this conclusion, that a certain book comes from God, and is invested with his authority ; but it does not suppose either knowledge of its contents or adoption of them. The rational believer, when he has rationally believed, has, after all, a *real* faith to seek, a faith that shall be good for anything, here or hereafter.

Let us now turn to the other side, and imagine a man who is no rational believer, but has only a dim idea that the Bible may be divine ; or even a fixed conviction that it is not divine, but merely human. He opens and reads, and as he reads, he is brought to a sudden pause, and is irresistibly impelled to think—"God is here and I knew it not." (I speak that which I do know, I simply record that of which I have the highest proof.) It is, as if the Invisible whispered in the deepest depth of his nature, "I have found thee, and thou mayst no more escape." A preternatural touch goes to the quick of his soul, and it trembles. Reason within him, and conscience, wake up to life and say, "It is true, read again ; it is there, it is true, it is divine." A voice from within answers to the voice without, and the conviction is instant, irresistible—"this is God, be sure of it ; this is God." The Bible meets, wakes up, answers to the divine intuitions of the soul, the deep longings, wants, sufferings, sins, fears and hopes of man ! Answers to them, and exceeds them all, reveals wants unfelt before, creates longings that never stirred before, sheds light, higher, purer, brighter, more ravishing, than the eye ever caught a glimpse of before, finds and draws forth intuitions in the silence of the reason and conscience which had lain dormant ever before, and shows other and higher points of vision, glorious peaks, hidden from the unaided eye, glancing in the blended radiance of wisdom, purity, truth, power, and love. *This* is the majesty and might of self-attestation, *this* is evidence, whose force falls on the educated and uneducated, on him who has searched into the external proofs, and on him who knows nothing of them ; *this* is evidence which it is pitiful and poor to call positive ; it is more than positive, it is invincible, it is almighty, and carries the conviction triumphantly to our heart of hearts ; "This is from above, only and wholly, and for ever divine."

There are some grave difficulties which will be instantly suggested in great force, to certain minds, by statements like these. What need of revelation, they will eagerly ask, if reason already contains within itself all that is supposed to be revealed ?   But reason does not contain all that is supposed to be revealed. This is not asserted. Quite the reverse. But reason contains truth *akin* to that which is revealed ; it is *the place* of such truth, of ultimate, native intuitions, it is the power through which we recognize and take hold of the divine, which revelation makes known. There is then, it may be urged, no supreme authority, no infallible judge such as we have been in the habit of supposing the inspired Scriptures to be.   Reason would seem to be exalted above revelation, at all events placed on a level with it.   Every man becomes on these principles, his own highest authority, and accepts or rejects what he pleases, according to the dictates of his reason, and con-science, and that, *practically*, must amount to his own whim and caprice, at different times, and in different states of mind.

There *is* danger, always, and in everything however apparently safe. The soundest principles, the surest truths, are not secure against danger. There is great danger from the pride of reason, from the vanity, the stiff dogmatism, the stubborn selfhood of men, from fanaticism, from superstition, and from the tendency to a false mysticism in superior minds. Let the danger be guarded against, with the most jealous and untiring care. But it is not inevitable. Surely, there may be a cautious, a wise, a humble, a self-distrusting, a reverent, a godly use of the powers, with which, for the noblest ends, our Maker has endowed us.

As it is, we must not overlook, either the existing fact of a diversity of Christian opinions, almost endless, or the humiliating lessons which it teaches. The immense number of Protestant and of Romish sects, reveal what must ever be the inevitable result, so long as the sphere is open to different minds. Nothing can be more decisive than the motto of all the evangelical churches, " the scriptures of the Old and New Testaments, the only infallible rule of faith and manners." But free-will and necessity, resistible and irresistible grace, election and non-election, universal atonement and limited atonement, salvation of infants and perdition, eternity and non-eternity of evil—

not to name points far more widely apart still—are all based on the one infallible authority.

The question is quite apart, how does revelation, viewed differently, as it inevitably must be, by different minds, *best* authenticate its origin ? I have sought to answer the question on the ground of facts, patent, outcrying, innumerable facts, which seem to admit of no interpretation but one. The entire mass of the Christian laity, especially the Christian commonalty, know, and can know next to nothing of external proofs, they have and can have nothing, but the internal, self-attesting evidence. I maintain that *this* is enough ; *they* have found it abundantly enough, rationally indestructible. And every real accepter of revelation, though he have first inquired into the external seals of its divine origin, must come *to this*, also, at last, and can rest only here.

We say, and rightly say, that so much letter-press within two boards, contains the message from heaven. But practically, and in effect, each man's bible is so much as he has found and put within him, and no more. He may find, he ought to find, ever more and more, but that only which he *has* found, is *the* revelation to him. The rest is a bible only in name. A mine is opened before us ; it is filled with treasure, and is inexhaustible. But my wealth consists only of so much genuine metal as I find and make my own and carry with me, and put to use. Others find what I do not, and I may find what they have missed. It is open to all, it belongs to all alike, but each is rich only in that which he gets possession of. The best test of a gold mine is the actual finding of gold in it. Geologists, mineralogists, and practical workmen may survey a district and may predict that gold must be found there. But to dig and find gold, to dig still, and find more gold, settles all questions, and makes doubt impossible. *Finding the Divine* puts the stoutest unbelief to flight, and the Divine which we find is *our* Bible, no more. The self-attesting divinity of revelation, its inherent life and force, form its best evidence. Valuable, indispensable as the external proof is, in its own place, *this* is it which has made Christianity omnipotent, has secured its noblest triumphs, and spread its sweeping conquests. It is power. It touches the soul, comes home to the deepest thoughts and feelings, and far transcends them and inspires the conviction of its own assured divinity.

And shall we then suspect and distrust reason and conscience ; that higher nature within us, through which, through which alone, we have come near to the Invisible indwelling spirit of Revelation, and which is even specially constituted to recognize this Holy Presence ? Shall we suspect and distrust it, as if it were the foe and not the ally of scripture ? If *we* do, the Great Being does not. Are we wiser, more thoughtful, more prudent than *he ?* Low and feeble, as our nature, confessedly is, and often fallacious, *He* has trusted it, most marvellously. Through this and only this, it has been shown already, anterior to revelation. He summons us, to rise to the idea of Himself; through this and only this. He has left us to reach the conception of His intelligent, free, moral being. By the aid of this, and only this, we are first of all in a condition to look into what claims to be a revelation from him, and when the revelation is in our hands, it is *this* chiefly, though not alone, which the revelation addresses. As for the claim of divinity, made by revelation, we have no means—the world, with the exception of a few among the privileged, educated classes—has no possible means of testing it, save through this and only this. It is this, this alone which finds the Invisible *in* the message, and summons us to adore and believe.

We MIGHT afford to dispense with all the external evidences, on which Mr. Mansell relies so much. But the internal, self-attesting divinity, we *could not* afford to lose. Were this to go, all would go. There would then be no God to us ; we could not recognize him, could not answer to his voice, his touch. There would then remain to us, only darkness and death—death to all that is most real within us and above us !

CHAPTER III.

REVELATION AND GOD.

I THINK, I am not wrong in asserting, that the Bampton Lecture is the first and only book, in any language, which maintaining the doctrine of a revelation from Heaven, at the same time, denies that the revelation reveals God. That it actually does so, it will be possible to make exceedingly plain. I am not conscious of anything, but an act of perfect fairness and justice, when the lecturer is represented as maintaining, that *something* is revealed in the scriptures, but it is not God, not God *as He is*, and when it is concluded that if so, we are shut up to the alternative that it is God *as He is not* ; for God, somehow, it certainly is. *The* thing of all things, which is unrevealed and incapable of being revealed, is God, that is, very God. Whatever be the purpose of the Old and New Testaments, to reveal God, the true, very God, to bring him forth to his creatures, *as He really is* and as he alone can be truly conceived, is not included in that purpose. Perhaps his meaning is nowhere expressed so shortly, nakedly and unequivocally, as in a note in his second lecture (p. 305), where he refers to " the admission, which is ultimately forced on us, that our human conception of *the Infinite* is NOT the TRUE one." The Infinite is God, or it is nothing. The Infinite, with the lecturer, is God, and God is the Infinite. What is true of the one, he holds to be true of the other—rightly or wrongly is not the question. The Infinite is simply and only a synonym for God, and the sentence quoted is virtually this, " our human conception of God is *not the true one.*"

Altogether, a preliminary remark is needed in reference to such phrases as Infinite, Absolute nature, the Absolute God, God in his absolute essence, and so forth. Already notice has been taken of this phraseology. But the notice must be repeated. " The Absolute God," most persons would conceive to mean the true God, very God, and so understood, its use would be quite harmless. But the philosophical sense is perfectly different ; it is the absolved God, God loosed from all relation, *The Unconditioned.* It has been shown, that there is no unconditioned, Absolute God, no absolute essence, and there never was to any rational creature. The God of consciousness, the true God, is a voluntarily conditioned being, standing in direct relation to his creatures. The Absolute, therefore, applied to God, is not simply unmeaning, it is positively false. The entire phraseology, borrowed from a philosophy, which is wholly idealistic, is to be utterly condemned and discarded. In like manner, it has been shown, that the term Infinite, applies strictly to the eternal duration of God. *That* is Infinite. But beyond this, men have no right to apply terms of their own coining to the Great Being. In all aspects of his nature, He is incapable of limit, past finding out, above the highest conceptions of his highest creatures. But this is the utmost that any are entitled to assert. The Bampton lecturer, however, maintains a perfectly opposite view. To him God is the Absolute, the Infinite, His essence is the absolute essence. Rightly or wrongly is not the question here. But this is the fact—he applies these phrases to God, he uses them as synonymous with God, and what he asserts in reference to them, he is to be understood as asserting in reference to God, the living God—otherwise his whole reasoning is purposeless. I understand this, and shall act entirely on this understanding. No one can legitimately understand anything else.

In order that the amplest justice may be done and a perfectly faithful impression made, in reference to the point before us, I shall first of all quote *en masse*, the whole of the passages, of which afterwards I shall have to make separate use. He speaks of "the morbid horror of *anthropomorphism*, which poisons the speculations of so many modern philosophers, when they attempt to be wise above what is written, and seek for a *metaphysical exposition* of God's nature and attributes. They may not, *forsooth*, think of the unchangeable God, as if He were *their fellow-man*, influenced by *human* motives and moved by *human* supplications. They want a truer, juster idea of the Deity *as He is*, than that under which He has been pleased to reveal Himself, and they call on their reason to furnish it. Fools, to dream that man can *escape from himself*, that human reason can draw aught but *a human portrait* of God . . . . do we ascribe to Him a fixed purpose ? Our conception of a purpose is human. Do we speak of Him as *continuing unchanged ?* Our conception of continuance is human. Do we conceive Him as knowing and determining ? What are knowledge and determination but *modes of human consciousness ?*" (pp. 17–18.) " Revelation can make known the Infinite Being, only in one of two ways, by *presenting* Him *as He is*, or by *representing* Him under symbols more or less adequate." (p. 27.) " Revelation represents the Infinite God, under *finite symbols*, in condescension to the finite capacity of man . . . . rationalism claims to behold God *as He is now;* it finds a common object for religion and philosophy, in the *explanation* of God." (p. 31.) " We feel that though God is indeed, in his incomprehensible essence, absolute and infinite; it is not *as the absolute and infinite*, that He appeals to the love, and the fear, and the reverence of his creatures. We feel that the *life* of religion lies in the human relations in which God reveals Himself to man, *not* in the *divine* perfections, which those relations *veil and modify*, though without *wholly* concealing. We feel that the God to whom we pray and in whom we trust, is *not so much* the God *eternal and infinite*, without body, parts, or passions (though we acknowledge He is all these), as the God who is gracious and merciful, etc." (pp. 64–65.) " To have sufficient grounds for believing in God is a very different thing from having sufficient grounds for reasoning about Him ; . . . . the natural senses, it may be, are diverted and colored by the medium through which they pass, to reach the intellect, and present to us, not things *in themselves*, but things as they appear to us. And this is manifestly *the case* with *the religious consciousness*, which can only represent the Infinite God, through finite forms. But we are compelled to believe, on the evidence of our senses, that a *material world exists*, even while we listen to the arguments of the idealist, who reduces it to *an idea* or *a nonentity*, and we are *compelled by our religious consciousness* to believe in the existence of a personal God, though the reasonings of the rationalist logically followed out, may *reduce us to Pantheism or Atheism.*" (p. 122.)   "The first mode aims at a speculative knowledge of God *as He is ;* . . . . the second, abandoning the speculative knowledge of the Infinite, ... is content with *those regulative* ideas of the Deity, which are sufficient to *guide our practice,* but not to *satisfy our intellect,* which tell us *not what God is Himself,* but how *He wills that we should* think of Him. . . . . He knows that human worship is not incompatible with infinite wisdom and goodness, though it is *not as the Infinite* that God reveals Himself in his moral government, *nor is it as the Infinite* that He promises to answer prayer." (pp. 126–8.)   "In this manifestation of God to man, alike in consciousness as in Scripture, *under finite forms* to *finite minds,* as a person to a person, we see the root and foundation of that religious service, without which *belief is a speculation* and worship a delusion."   (p. 128.)   "It is, then, strictly in analogy with the method of God's providence, if we believe He has given us truths, *intended not to satisfy* our reason, but to guide our practice ; *not to tell us* what God *is* in his *absolute nature,* but *how He wills that we should* think of Him in our present state."   (p. 143.)   "It is to be expected that our knowledge of God, *though revealed by Himself*, is revealed *in relation* to human faculties, and *subject to* the *limitations and imperfections*, inseparable from the constitution of the human mind." (p. 144.) "We may believe and ought to believe that the conceptions which *we are compelled* to adopt as the guides of our thoughts and actions now, may, indeed, in the sight of a higher intelligence, be but partial truth, but *cannot be total falsehood.*" (p. 145.) "We must remain content with the belief, that we have *that knowledge of* God which is best adapted to our wants and training. *How far* that knowledge represents God, *as He is*, we know not and have no need to know." (p. 146.) "*The true conception* of the Divine nature, *so far as we are able* to receive it, is to be found in those regulative representations which exhibit God *under limitations, accommodated* to the constitution of man, not in the *unmeaning abstractions*, which, aiming at a higher knowledge, distort rather than exhibit the Absolute and the Infinite." (p. 150.) "We cannot help observing, how the Almighty, in communicating with his people, condescends to place Himself on what, humanly speaking, may be called *a lower level* than that on which *the natural reason of man* would be inclined to exhibit Him." (p. 152.) "The Father has *revealed Himself* to mankind, *under human types and images*, that He may appeal more earnestly and effectually to man's *consciousness of the human spirit* within him. The Son has done more than this. He became, for our sakes, very man ; . . . . being both God and man. Herein is our justification, if we refuse to aspire beyond those limits of human thought in which He placed us. Here is our answer, if any man would spoil us through philosophy and vain deceit. *Is it rational* to contemplate God, under symbols drawn from *the human consciousness?* Christ is our pattern, for in Him dwelleth all the fulness of the Godhead bodily." (p. 154.)

It would be difficult to find an instance of anything more fatuitous in reasoning than is supplied by the last of these quotations. The very words, "in him dwelt all the fulness of the godhead bodily," contain the instant answer to the fallacious inferences of the lecturer. Who ever thought, or said, that it was "irrational to contemplate God under symbols drawn from the human consciousness ?" Whence, else, could they be drawn ? But the question is, whether symbols drawn from the human consciousness, or elsewhere, do truly, or only fallaciously, represent God, whether they bring us down to themselves, or prompt us, and help us to rise above themselves. The Redeemer of men was man ; are we therefore, taught to think of the Almighty as man, are we not, on the contrary, impelled, from man, through man, by the aid of man, to rise to God. The Redeemer of men was man ; but his humanity suggested, uttered, imaged more than the human, because it included more than the human, because it was the temple of the indwelling Deity. Had the purpose been to keep us down to the human, a common humanity had sufficed. But a common humanity did not suffice. A superhuman humanity was set before the world ; a divine humanity, one in which dwelt the fulness of Godhead —just that we might be saved from abiding with the notion of mere human attributes and modes, and might be compelled, in thought, to ascend to divine excellences. Jesus spake as man never spake, acted as man never acted, lived as man never lived, and died as man never died. A mysterious sovereignty, not human, rested upon him, a purity, a wisdom, a forgivingness, a gentleness, a power of endurance and of self-sacrifice, a patience, a meekness, and a love, which were not only symbols of the divine, but were themselves verily divine. Anthropomorphism is harmless when it guides the human to transcend itself, when it lifts it up to the idea of a superhuman perfection. It is dangerous and blasphemous when it seeks to bring down God to the level of his creatures, and conceives their weaknesses and limitations as also His.

This levelling of the Divine, in my humble judgment, is the intent and drift of the Bampton lecture ; it distinctly aims to justify anthropomorphism, on philosophical grounds. How else, shall we account for the bitter contempt with which, in one of the passages already quoted, the lecturer speaks of " the morbid horror of anthropomorphism" —as if it were not at all a thing to be afraid of— " which poisons the speculations of so many modern philosophers when they attempt to be wise above what is written, and seek for a metaphysical exposition of the nature and attributes of God." By the way, only by the way, it is possible to seek a knowledge of God's nature and attributes, without desiring that it be metaphysical, far less that it shall consist of what, in another passage, the lecturer calls, " unmeaning abstractions, which distort rather than exhibit God." The two things are quite apart, and not without great injustice are they here conjoined. A knowledge, a true, not a fallacious, knowledge of God is what we seek. The lecturer continues, " they"—those who have a horror of anthropomorphism—" may not, *forsooth*, think of the unchangeable God, as if he were their fellow man, influenced by human motives, and moved by human supplications." This piece of not well-timed irony can only mean that what these men think they may not do, the lecturer thinks they may and ought to do—it is their fault that they do not. It must mean, that we ought to conceive of God, as if he were our fellow man, influ-

enced and moved as human beings are influenced
and moved. He continues—"Fools, to dream that
man can escape from himself, that human reason
can draw aught but a human portrait of God."

What *man* does, or thinks, is human, must be
human, never can be anything but human. But
whether a man's thought can carry a man above
man's self, is not touched. Man is always man ;
what he does is man's doing, what he thinks is
man's thinking, is human. In this sense he can
never transcend himself. Is this what the lecturer
means ? If so, there is some room for an honest
indignation against what is surely not fit treatment of a solemn and great subject. Has any one,
in his right mind, thought or said that man could
be not man ? I must call this worse than trifling.
The lecturer continues—"do we ascribe to God a
fixed purpose, our conception of a purpose is human—do we speak of Him as continuing unchanged,
our conception of continuance is human—do we
conceive him as knowing and determining, what
are knowledge and determination but modes of human consciousness."

I am quite unable to make anything else of these
questions and answers than this, that they are a
very philosophical, very learned mode of stating a
very plain fact, namely, that man is always man,
that when he speaks about God, or anything else,
he uses human words, because he has none other to

use ; and when he conceives anything, his conception is a human conception, simply because he *is* a man, and not an angel ; and when he thinks, his thought is a human thought, that is to say, it is formed by a human mind, and according to those laws that guide and govern human thinking. But the question is not touched at all, whether the human thought may be a correct thought or no, whether it may answer truly, to that with which it is occupied. Schelling alone, in the philosophic circle, with whom the mystics of earlier and of later times are substantially at one, asserts the possibility of transcending consciousness. But were he silenced, as on this point he easily can be, the question would be as far as ever from being determined, whether within the limits of consciousness, and according to the formal laws of thought, it be possible for the human mind to rise to that which is superhuman, to think of it, and to think accurately and truly. This question, the only one at issue, is not touched by the lecturer. I maintain that the laws of thought and of consciousness, the spiritual constitution of man, established by the Great Maker, are such, as to show a divine intention that man *should* be able to escape from himself, that human reason should be able to draw more than a human portrait, aye, many a portrait of *superhuman* excellence and greatness, and that the human mind should be able to rise to that which is far above itself. I maintain it, on the ground of experience and of fact. The lecturer may taunt those whom he calls dreaming fools, and may lash them with his bitterest irony. But, perhaps, they have no cause to be much moved. It is more than an adequate compensation to them, that *they* are able, and know and feel that they are able, to conceive power, and wisdom, and rectitude, and perfection, which it would be contradictory to attach to any mere humanity. It is no question with them. They are *conscious* of power to conceive a superhuman spiritual nature, in which superhuman attributes and excellences reside. Man *can* escape from himself, can transcend himself, he is constituted to transcend himself, far and farther and yet farther still, to rise above himself, and nearer and nearer to the Great Being.

We meet in the Bampton Lecturer, constant reference to " the finite forms, finite symbols, and human types and images of Holy Scripture, and to the condescension to finite capacities, and the accommodation to the limitations and imperfections, inseparable from the constitution of the human mind." One is tempted to ask, Who ever heard or dreamt of infinite forms, or infinite symbols, or types, or images, who ever heard of infinite words, who ever dreamt of such ? The constant repetition is startling. Without any such intention, on the part of the writer, it goes to create an impression, quite apart from argument. Man *is* a finite being, in the midst of finite beings and things. But the constant and utterly useless repetition and reiteration of the word finite is apt, in certain minds, to nourish a prejudice, a pre-judgment, of the question, "Whether, through the finite, man can ascend to that which is far above the finite, to the conception of the living God, of whom infinity is one of the distinguishing attributes." Of course, in speaking of this Great Being, revelation employs, the only materials which are possible, finite words, forms, types, and images, and at last a finite human nature, the man Christ Jesus, who was God as well as man. But the use of all these is, not that we should rest *in them*, but that we should conceive that which is immeasurably above them, that which they are intended to suggest and strike out.

On the whole, there seems to be an entire misapprehension, pervading this portion of the Bampton Lecture, with respect to the proper meaning and use of an image or symbol. For illustration, let us take a very frequent phrase—"mental growth." The words are figurative, typical. The question is, is it intended that I am to bind my thought down to the actual symbol, or am I to use it as a ladder for ascending to what is above it? Here, in the literal image, we have first ; ground properly prepared and manured, then a seed deposited in it, the seed is saturated with mois-

ture and warmed by the sun, it softens, fer-
ments, decays, perishes, a green sprout gradually
breaks out, it elongates, thickens, strikes up and
up, grows stronger and stronger. Have I to keep
my thought down to these and such things? Or,
on the contrary, forgetting them all, in themselves,
have I only to use them, as helps for suggesting
something totally different *in kind*, where there is no
soil, no manure, no rain, no moisture, no sun, no fer-
mentation, no sprouting. I must rise, if I would
understand and make intelligent use of the figure,
I must rise to a purely spiritual nature, the idea of
the gradual increase of knowledge, the gradual filling and furnishing the mind, the gradual awakening
and exercising, and invigoration of the powers, the
implantation and strengthening and progress of inward principles. The types and images of scripture are only degraded (any types and images
would be only degraded and perverted) if we bind
our thought down to the actual form. The entire
end of the most sacred symbols is destroyed, if we
put *them* in the place of that, which they are to
signify and suggest. True, they are human, finite,
in condescension to our capacity, in accommodation to our limited nature. True, most true, as
the lecturer says, "The Father has revealed himself to mankind under human types and images,
that he may appeal more earnestly and effectually,
to man's consciousness of the human spirit within

him." Is there any other than a human spirit within him, to which an appeal could be made ; why have we this labored, repetitious, pleonastic ringing out of the terms, human, finite, as if we were in danger of forgetting that man is man. The Merciful Father does indeed seek to touch, in the nearest, closest, tenderest possible way, the consciousness of his creatures, by means of images which they can at once understand and feel. But is it, that they should only keep to these images, is it not, rather, that they should rise above them? That is the question. The human type has a superhuman reality, to which it answers, which it is meant to suggest to us. It is used, *not* for its own sake. We abuse, we pervert, we destroy it, if we put *it* in the place of the higher reality. Its whole intention is to lift us up to what is above it. An image is an image of something, and the something above it which it images and not itself, is the end of its use.

" We cannot help observing," says the lecturer, " how the Almighty in communicating with his creatures, condescends to place himself in what humanly speaking, may be called a lower level, than that on which the natural reason of man would be inclined to exhibit him." In the name of the natural reason and its almighty inspirer, this is utterly denied. The words are denied, but much more the spirit they breathe. If there be

any one thing in the bible, more than another, to
which the natural reason of man clings, it is its
simple, human, touching imagery. And why?
Because, of all things, the soul finds *this* to be
mightily helpful, in inspiring the truest, loftiest,
divinest thoughts of the Great Being. Were we
to rest in the imagery itself, instead of allowing it
to lift us, as it is intended it should lift us, to what
is far above it, then, indeed, the Almighty *would
be* placed, on a lower level. And *this*, it has been
shown, *this* is what the lecturer does and counsels
all to do.

Respecting the nature of revelation, the views
expressed by Mr. Mansell are strangely unfixed,
apparently unpremeditated. " Revelation, it is
said, can make known the Infinite Being, only in
one of two ways, by *presenting* Him *as He is*, or
by *representing* him under symbols more or less
adequate." This sounds acute and elegant, but it
is without foundation. *Present* God ? *Present*,
in distinction from *represent ?* We present a living being, *in person* and in no other way that I
know of. We represent him in words or by signs
of one kind or other. Revelation cannot *present*
God at all, the idea is preposterous and absurd ;
and I am by no means sure, that this is the only
instance in which sense has been sacrificed to sound.
Revelation can do nothing but represent God. The
representation is thought to be, it calls itself, a re-

velation, an unveiling. At all events, it is a representation of God, in words and by images and types. Is the representation *true*, or *false?* That is a great question! The verdict of the lecturer upon it is hardly doubtful. He does, indeed, seem to say—in fact, he does say—that God reveals himself, but he verily means conceals, not reveals— "The life of religion lies in the human relations in which God reveals himself to man, *not in the divine perfections*, which those relations *veil* and modify, though without wholly concealing." How God reveals—*i. e., un*veils—Himself, in relations which *veil* His divine perfections, few could pretend to understand. To the same effect is the passage relating to the evidence of the senses :—" The natural senses, it may be, are diverted and colored by the medium through which they pass to reach the intellect and present to us *not things in themselves*, but things as they appear to us. And *this* is manifestly *the case* with the religious consciousness," &c. If this does not mean that our external senses are partly fallacious and deceptive, and that, like them, *our religious consciousness* is also partly *fallacious* and *deceptive*, what can it mean ?

Revelation *represents* God to mankind, and there are manifestly only two senses in which it *can* do so—either truly or untruly. Truly or untruly? —that is the great question. The Bampton lecturer, not once, but times without number, vehemently resists the idea that God is or can be re-presented *as He is.* Can there be an alternative but this, that He must then be represented *as He is not?* Quite in consistency with this alternative, we read of "those regulative ideas of the Deity, which are sufficient to guide our practice, but not to satisfy our intellect; of truths *intended* not to satisfy our reason, but to guide our practice." The scriptures "tell us, *not* what God is *in Himself,* but *how He wills* that we should think of Him; they are intended to tell us not what God is *in his absolute nature,* but *how He wills* that we should think of Him in our present state." On the whole, it is as plain as very intelligible words can make it, that for our sakes God is represented *not as He is,* but *as He is not.* The knowledge communicated to us is not the true knowledge, but only "that which is best adapted to our wants and our training." The deliberate judgment of the lecturer is expressed in the following decisive sentences :—"How far that knowledge (given in the scriptures) represents God *as He is*—in other words, *truly* represents God—we *know not.*" "Our conceptions of God, the conceptions *we are compelled* to adopt, may, indeed, be but partial truth, but they cannot be *total falsehood.*" "Our human conception of the Infinite," of God who alone is the Infinite, "is *not the true one.*" This is the verdict on the awful question—"Not True," yet "Not Total Falsehood ;" How far true, or How far false, " we know not." I end as I began ; something is revealed, but it is *not God*. *The* thing of all things, which is unrevealed and incapable of being revealed, is God.

It is a lamentable result ! The worship of all Christian churches and congregations, the prayers of all good Christian people, are offered up to *the* unknown Being. We cannot trust our religious consciousness, for, like our bodily senses, it is a coloring, if not distorting medium, through which objects cannot be presented as they are in themselves. We cannot trust divine revelation, for its representations are intentionally not true, though not total falsehood ; they teach us, indeed, the mode in which God *wills that we should* think of Him, but we know that that mode is *not true*, though how far it is from the truth we know not. The deep moan of a troubled human heart is wafted across the dark expanse of three thousand years—" O that I knew where I might find Him, that I might come even to His seat !" And in the long interval many and many a spirit in like trouble has lifted up the same burdened cry. There is no answer to it, on the principles with which we have been contending ; no answer, save one, which it were merciful to withhold. " You cannot find *Him ;* you cannot know *Him*. Something you may know, something you may find, but *not, never,* the true, the real God."

But there *is* an answer to the question, of a very different character, and from a very different quarter. "We know that the Son of God has come and hath given us an understanding *to know* Him that is true." "This is life eternal, that they might *know* thee, the only true God and Jesus Christ, whom thou hast sent." "Every one that loveth is born of God and *knoweth* God. He that loveth not knoweth not God, for God *is* love."

An *ideal counterpart*, in us, compressing Infinity within the limits of our minds, is impossible. It is admitted in the fullest extent. But has the Great Being no godlike ways, thoughts, utterances that proclaim him at once, that bring him truly before our thoughts, far more truly than if we had a visible representation before our eyes? It is distressing, profoundly distressing, in my humble judgment, if our experience compels us, for ourselves, to answer, No. Yet more distressing, if to others, in reply to their eager questioning, we are compelled to answer, No.

There was one who could, and did, proclaim, "He that hath seen me hath seen the Father"— the invisible through the visible. Many a time, the Divinity broke through his humanity; as when he spoke to the guilty woman—"Daughter, doth no man condemn thee? neither do I condemn thee ; go, and sin no more ;" or, when on the cross he prayed, " Forgive them, for they know not what they do ;" or, when on the mountain side, he taught the multitudes, " Blessed are the poor in spirit, for theirs is the kingdom of heaven ;" " blessed are the pure in heart, for they shall see God." Never *man* spake *so*. God was *in* such words, and breathes out of them, at this moment, on the world, with the glow of unutterable wisdom and love. "I thank thee, oh Father, that hast revealed to babes the things hidden from the wise and prudent."

SECTION FIFTH.

CONCERNING MORALITY AND A MORAL SENSE.

CHAPTER I.

THE RELATIVE AND THE REAL.

Relation to Faculties of Knower—Phenomena—Also Noumena—Ground to Believe this—Consciousness not Fallacious—Knowing Faculty not Fallacious—Minds generically the same—Limited, not therefore Unreal.

THE question as to the relativity or reality of all our knowledge, lies very near to that which touches specially our connection with the Great Being. There are strong peculiarities attaching to the latter, which render it, in some degree, independent of other questions. But the scepticism—I can call it by no other name—which denies that we can know God *as he is*, belongs to that wider scepticism which denies that we can know anything *as it is*. Sorrowfully it must be confessed, that *here*, not only Kant but Hamilton is at one with the Bampton lecturer. And the position which they in common maintain, it must be granted, seems to be *logically* unassailable. Yet I hope to be able to make out that, in effect and in fact, it is not sound, and that all which is ascertainable by logic is not all which is ascertainable by other means.

Here are some of the modes in which formal

science puts its unwelcome result :—" We can know only as we have faculties for knowing." " Not that which *is*, can we reach, but only that which is in some way relative, analogous to our powers, and only so far as it is relative to our powers." " *Quicquid recipitur, recipitur ad modum recipientis.*" " Things as they appear to us, but not things as they are in themselves—phenomena, not noumena, are for us." " Of existence absolutely and in itself we know nothing."

Perhaps it is not much to say, that all this is strongly opposed to the ordinary convictions of mankind. Most men would be disposed to assert with confidence, We *must*, we *do*, we *certainly* do know, at least, *some* things *in themselves ;* we know them really, not simply as they appear to us, but as they *must* appear to all intelligent beings, and that is, as they really are in themselves. There may not be much in this fact, but in the event of independent presumptive reasons being discovered, tending in the same direction, it *is* something to have this strong background of general conviction on which to lean.

One thing is quite certain, we *can* know only so much and so far as we have faculties for knowing. Were our faculties strengthened, were they more numerous, as we can well imagine them to be, the sphere of our knowledge would be indefinitely enlarged. That is to say, our knowledge, at present, is certainly limited. But who denies that it is? It is undeniable. Of any subject, in any direction, we know only so much. With no great stretch of fancy we can imagine our knowledge, in every direction, to be immensely increased. But limited knowledge, so far as it goes, need not be therefore untrustworthy, it may be perfectly reliable and real. We can know only what appears to us, and what is relative to our faculties. But because a thing appears to us and is related to our faculties, is it *just therefore* not real and actual, in itself? Who has demonstrated this? It has never been, it cannot be demonstrated. Here, it would appear, lies the fallacy, at all events the defect, in the theory which maintains the relativity, not in distinction from, but as opposed to the reality, of all our knowledge. It takes for granted that phenomena, just because they are phenomena, are therefore not noumena. But this is not proved, cannot be proved. Phenomena may not be, also, noumena; the two are quite apart. Granted. But there is nothing to hinder that they *be*, also, noumena. This has never been disproved, cannot be disproved. When it is asserted, " We can know *only* phenomena," even logically, the position is not strictly defensible. We *do* know phenomena— what we know are phenomena—THAT is certain; logic is entitled to affirm it. But logic cannot legitimately add a single word. That we know *only*

phenomena, in other words, that the phenomena
are only phenomena, is a gratuitous assumption.
Certain things, in reference to matter, and in reference to mind, *appear*, of which we can and do take
hold. But may not the things which appear *be
the* things themselves. I maintain that there is no
reason to think anything else, and very strong presumptive reasons to lead us to think *this*. Knowledge, though limited, may, so far as it goes, be
perfectly reliable. It is of phenomena, but it need
not therefore be of mere phenomena, in distinction
from realities. The actual things themselves may
appear to us—why not ? and thus be both phenomena and noumena.

Let us turn for illustration to the power of consciousness. This is the one essential condition of
all intellectual activity. I know, only as I know
that I know ; I feel, only as I know that I feel ; I
desire and will, only as I know that I desire and
will. This is the light of all our seeing, the light,
in which all our mental states and acts are visible
to the eye of the soul. With what is my thought
occupied at this moment ? what emotion is passing
through me ? what desire, or volition, is forming ?
This, and *this*, and *this* : I know it, I am conscious
of it, it admits of no doubt. We cannot go higher.
The testimony of consciousness is accepted, as indubitable. It is the ultimate authority, from which
there is no appeal. Kant, Hamilton, and Mansell,

bow to it. It is the one, only, foundation of philosophy. The testimony of consciousness, as a revelation of the facts of our inward being, *must* be accepted, unconditionally, else philosophy is no longer possible. It *is* accepted. But why, on what ground ? Simply because we cannot believe, and have no ground to believe, quite otherwise, that our nature is a lie. But this is to fall back, not so much on ourselves, as on our Creator. In constituting and constructing our nature, he cannot have meant us to believe a falsehood, cannot have erected within us a lying witness.

We are entitled, I think, to apply the same mode of reasoning in other special cases. Here, for example, my faculty of knowing belongs to the structure of my nature, quite as much as my consciousness does. If I accept the latter as no deception, no falsehood palmed upon me, why should I any more distrust the former. True, I know only what appears to my faculty of knowing, what it is formed to take hold of. If it did not *appear*, and were wholly unrelated to my mind, it would be to me nothing. But *because* it appears, does it, therefore, become nothing, and is it to be counted by me for no reality ? I think the highest reason is at one with the strong natural convictions of mankind generally, in the conclusion that our knowledge is real, though it be relative ; real, though it be phenome-

nal ; not *merely* phenomenal, but also noumenal—
the two being perfectly consistent.

Logic is a stern authority, and logic asserts,
" what you know are phenomena," and logic cannot make out that phenomena, in any case, are also
realities.   But there may be strong ground, nevertheless, to believe it, and to believe it confidently.
Here is a book before me—I perceive it, I am conscious of perceiving, of knowing it.   It *appears* to
me ; .if it did not, I could know nothing about it.
It *is* a phenomenon, but I know that it *is more*,
my knowing faculty declares it to be a real, substantial existence, a fact in God's universe.   It is
not mere phenomenon.   It is a veritable something,
and I know it to be a veritable something, that is,
if I give credit to my power of knowing.   I *do*
know it *as it is*, not perfectly, not all comprehen-
sively.   But what I do know is actually true of it.
If I had ten senses, instead of five, or a hundred
instead of ten, I should discover properties that are
now hidden ; but those which I had already discovered, would not thereby be falsified, else my
whole nature would be falsified along with them,
my mental constitution would then be an organ-
ized deception.

We must know things, really, as they are in
themselves, must know them as other intelligent
beings know them.   They may know far more,
and other properties, than we do ; but what we

know must abide true also, and enter into the conception of the reality. I *do* know myself, my real, very self. I do know myself truly, so far as my knowledge goes. Self is a phenomenon of consciousness, but it is a reality beyond it, at the same time, which I certainly know. What I am to my own consciousness, that, also, I must be to other intelligences who look upon me. They may know more, but they cannot know *contrary* to what I do. Perfect, universal knowledge of self, or of anything else, I have not, but a knowledge real, positive, and reliable, I have. I *do*, I *must* know my actual thoughts, my principles, my tendencies, my motives, my aims, my character, that which makes me what I am, and distinguishes me from others. In the same way, there *must* be a knowledge real, though limited, of other living beings, as well as of self—a knowledge of their actual character, of their place in the scale of intellectual and moral worth. Beyond this, a real external universe is before us, real mountains, seas, forests, and skies, not projected from within, not created by our minds, or by any laws that guide our perception and our thinkings, but out from them, actual substantial facts—phenomenal, it is true, appearing to us, else we could know nothing of them, relative to our faculties, but not the less real in themselves. Beyond this still there is real truth for the inward eye, as well as a real universe for the outward eye. There are real truths, standing quite out from our faculties, independent of them, *appearing* to us, indeed, but themselves solid verities. There is a real living God, over all.

Mr. Mansell interposes a difficulty in the way of real knowledge, as distinguished from relative, for which not many are likely to be prepared. When we speak of knowing things in themselves, knowing them as they are, we mean that our knowledge of them is not owing *merely* to the instrument with which we think, but much more to what is *in* them, themselves, to what is outward and actual in them, of which we, with our minds, take hold. In other words, we mean, that *we* know them, in some degree, as *any other mind*, anywhere, must know them. An outer, independent reality must be virtually the same to all intelligences. But the Bampton lecturer finds and asserts that " I can imagine other minds, only by first assuming their likeness to my own." (p. 203.)   This assumption, it is contended, I have no right to make. As a matter of pure reason, we know nothing of any created minds, save human minds. We may conjecture, may imagine, on various presumptive grounds, such other existence, but we cannot know it, as a fact. Revelation makes known finite intelligences, not human, vast in number, perhaps of different, separate orders, and higher in the scale of creation than mankind. We accept the fact, but why, the lecturer will ask, should "human intelligence be made the representative of all intelligence?" Perhaps this is a case in which one question may best be answered by another, and we ask in reply, why not? If it be legitimate to rise from our own spiritual nature, to the Supreme, the Divine spiritual nature—and our Maker has left us no means but this of reaching the conception of Himself—it can scarcely be derogatory to other creatures, if we conceive of them through ourselves. It seems not unphilosophical, but on the contrary most congenial and congruous, to conceive of all created minds, as brothers, elder born and younger born, perhaps; endowed with varying powers, but *generically* the same. It is impossible for us to conceive of Mind, anywhere, of any order or grade, except as a power of knowing, feeling, and desiring, or willing. Differences in degree may be endless, but *generic* difference is inconceivable, without a destruction of our whole notion of mind. Can we imagine any created intelligence, thinking that two and two are six, that the sun moves round the earth, that the monarchy of Britain is a republic, that a man is not essentially the same identical person at fifty as he was at thirty, that responsibility does not mean that we are answerable to a superior authority? We cannot. These are things not only true to us, but true *in themselves*, which all minds must look

upon, essentially, in the same light. A higher intelligence might have a deeper insight into the
science of numbers, the laws of the material universe, the theory of government, the doctrine of
personal identity, and into the relation subsisting
between man and his Creator than we have, but
that which we know are true, could not be false to
him ; it would be true to him also. Much more
might be true, but this at least would abide true.
Our knowledge is not complete, not perfect, but it
is of actual, positive verities, without us, and independent of us, and of all ; it is of things as
they are, and are seen by all intelligences. The
phenomena of consciousness are not fallacies, our
powers are not meant to deceive us, but to guide
us in their measure to truth and reality. Things
appear to us, but if they were merely appearances
they would be implicit untruths. We are invol-
untarily bound by certain laws, in obedience to
which thoughts are formed. But our nature becomes a falsehood, and our Maker a deceiver, if
these laws be not intended, not to keep us back
from reality, but to help us more surely to reach
it. Had we higher faculties, we might know more,
but this ought not rationally to create the slightest
suspicion that the acquaintance with things which
we *do* possess is not valid. Our knowledge is relative, it must be relative to our faculties—all
knowledge is necessarily relative to the faculties of

the being who possesses it—but it is not, therefore, not real. It is phenomenal, but phenomena are phenomena of something actual behind them, which they phenomenize, and thereby reveal. It is limited—so is all created knowledge, the knowledge of the highest created intelligence that exists, or can be conceived to exist—but so far as it goes, it is reliable and genuine.

CHAPTER II.

FROM what has been advanced, it is sufficiently
apparent—the fact, indeed, is admitted on all
sides—that logic is not an instrument for the
discovery of *new* truth. Its proper and only
office is to eliminate what *is* and what *is not*
involved in certain assumed data. Existing truth,
truth already contained in the premises, it can
detect and expose. But with this its function
ceases. If the premises be *true*, the strictly logical inferences and deductions from them cannot be
assailed. But even when the premises are strictly
true, *that* may be also true which goes far beyond
them. For example, in the brief discussion with
which we were last occupied, the phenomena of consciousness constitute the entire sphere of our knowledge, and logic, therefore justly concludes that all
our knowledge is phenomenal; or, again, on the
ground that we can know only so far as we have

faculties for knowing, logic justly concludes that all our knowledge is relative to our faculties. This is clearly involved, and it is *all* that is involved in the premises. But logic does not and cannot assert that, because *this* is true, it is also the *whole* truth that can be ascertained on the subject. So far from this we have found that what are truly the *phenomena* of consciousness are also more than phenomena, are *the things* themselves, which, indeed, appear to us, since, unless they did, they would be to us nothing. We have found, besides, that *that* which is truly relative to our faculties, is so not because of some special peculiarity in our mental structure which gives its own form to all that reaches it, but because of *generic* characteristics which must be common to all intelligent beings. Our knowledge *is* phenomenal, and it *is* relative ; but, on other grounds, we are able to conclude that it is perfectly reliable at the same time, so far as it goes.

There is one region, above all others, where the *nature* of our knowledge is a matter of supreme importance. It is the region of moral truth. If our ideas of right and wrong be not, in their measure, *real ;* if they be owing to a molding and shaping power in us, and not to the things themselves ; if they do not answer truly, in their measure, to very realities, there is nothing stable for us evermore. In my humble judgment, had that portion of the Bampton Lecture relating to conscience and to the nature of morality, stood alone, and had all the other portions been faultless, *this* would have rendered the work dangerous, in a degree hardly to be estimated ; and all the more, as it comes from a professed and sincere advocate of Christianity, whose sentiments, therefore, are likely to be adopted, without suspicion and without examination, by great multitudes. These sentiments, as I humbly judge, tend to sap the foundations of the highest truth and of all rational faith.

It would be vain to think of a full discussion *here*, of the nature of virtue and of the theory of our moral sentiments. Yet both of these high questions are intimately related to the subject which is to occupy us. Is there such a thing as right and wrong, a distinct quality of our mental and of our outward acts, separate from wisdom, from utility, from beauty, from æsthetic fitness, not opposite to these properties, even congenial with them all, but perfectly distinct from them, above them, super-added to them ? And is there a part or power of our nature which takes hold of this distinct quality, perceives it, makes us at once conscious of it—a power, besides, which asserts a supreme authority from which there is no appeal, and imperatively commands and forbids ? To these questions I find both an affirmative and a negative answer in the Bampton Lecture—affirmative, inasmuch as it seems to consent to the conclusions of Butler; negative, inasmuch as the whole of the reasonings are in the face of these conclusions. The lecturer will be found to deny what Butler distinctly held: first, immutable right and wrong, apprehensible by man ; and, secondly, conscience as the inward witness and revealer of immutable right and wrong. The opening reference to Kant, in the beginning of the seventh lecture, is almost decisive of this point. Not many could have dealt with his magnificent thoughts as the lecturer has done. I quote the passage entire, as translated by Hamilton (Lect. i. 39), with only a few unimportant changes. It is from the concluding portion of the treatise on the practical reason.

"Two things there are which the oftener and the more steadfastly we contemplate, fill the mind with an ever new and ever rising admiration and reverence—the starry heaven above me, the moral law within me. After neither, as if it were hidden in darkness or in the immensity beyond the sphere of my vision, do I need to search and merely conjecture. Both I contemplate lying clear before me, and both I connect immediately with my consciousness of existence. The one departs from the place I occupy in the outer world of sense, expands beyond the bonds of imagination this connection of my body with worlds rising beyond worlds, and systems blending into systems, and protends it also into the illimitable times of their periodic movements, to its commencement and perpetuity. The other departs from my invisible self, from my personality, and represents me in a world truly infinite indeed, but whose infinity can be tracked out only by the intellect, with which also my connection, unlike the fortuitous relation I stand in to all worlds of sense, I am compelled to recognize as universal and necessary. In the former, the first view of a countless multitude of worlds annihilates, as it were, my importance as an animal product, which, after a brief—and that incomprehensible—endowment with the powers of life, is compelled to refund its constituent matter to the planet on which it grew, itself an atom in the universe. The other, on the contrary, elevates my worth as an intelligence, even without limit, and *this* through my personality, in which the moral law reveals a faculty of life, independent of my animal nature—nay, of the whole material world ; at least, if it be permitted to infer as much from the regulation of my being which a conformity with that law exacts ; proposing, as it does, my moral worth for the absolute end of my activity, conceding no compromise of its imperative to the necessitation of nature, and spurning, in its infinity, the conditions and boundaries of my present transitory life."

Sir William Hamilton is all admiring, genial sympathy with the German sage. He quotes the foregoing passage " for the soundness of its doctrine and for the natural and unsought-for sublimity of the expression." He, with Kant, was a believer in conscience and in immutable morality. But the Bampton lecturer only objects and censures, only wonders at the inconsistency, which first proves all our knowledge to be relative, and then a portion of it to be real. The inconsistency is palpable, and has been marked by a thousand eyes. The practical is separated from the pure reason by an essential distinction, apparently without sufficient ground and in defiance of logic. But it is a glorious inconsistency, it is a noble blunder—perhaps no blunder, but a magnificent truth, only reached not soon enough. True, majestically true, is the grand discovery, where he finds it ; but it is true, also, where he found it not. In the pure reason, as well as in the practical reason, lie divine intuitions, eternal, necessary truths. But as to the latter, at all events, the practical reason, conscience, as we should say, Kant, yielding to the force of his own consciousness, upheld the indwelling in man of immovable moral convictions and of a supreme moral authority. But the Bampton lecturer only pertinaciously stands by the fact of Kant's logical inconsistency. And it is quite true, as he asserts, that " the result of the critical philosophy (in the hands of Kant) as applied to the speculative side of human reason, was to prove the existence of certain necessary forms and laws of intuition and of thought, which *impart a corresponding character* to all the objects of which consciousness, intuitive or reflective, can take cognizance." (p. 200.)   But according to the same philosophy, certain moral ideas, he insists, are not merely " facts of *human* consciousness, *conceived under the laws* of human thought, but *absolute, transcendent realities*, implied in the conception of all reasonable beings, as such, and therefore independent of the law of time, and binding *not on man as man*, but on all possible intelligent beings, created and uncreated.   The moral reason is thus a source of absolute and unchangeable *realities*, while the speculative reason is concerned only with *phenomena*, or things *modified by* the constitution of the human mind." (p. 201.)

It is not my business to defend Kant. Let it be granted, that so far as he is concerned the criticisms now quoted are just.   But these criticisms throw additional light on the principles, undoubtedly maintained by the lecturer. The distinction which is *here* made, is broad and impassable, between *realities* and *phenomena*, or, as he varies the expression, things *modified* by our minds, between *realities* and facts of *human consciousness*, *realities* and things conceived under *the laws of human thought*, between truth and right for *man* and truth and right for *other intelligent beings*. He insists that the forms and laws of thought impose a character *of their own* on whatever is the object of consciousnéss, quite other than the thing itself. It brings back repulsively the hard image of " a mind cramped by its own laws and bewildered in the contemplation of its own forms." The fixed idea seems to be, that the laws of thought are so many rigid moulds, so many contracted grooves, into which thought, like fused metal, is run, and from which it receives a peculiar form, unlike everything else ; at least whether like or unlike anything else, or how far like and how far unlike, we can never know. Perhaps it would be more philosophical, more generous, certainly more honorable to the Creator, to conceive of the forms of thought, as mirrors, so constructed and so set that by their mould and their position, they may, in their measure, reflect on us a truthful image of the realities that fall on their surface. On the lecturer's supposition, our minds must for ever present to us self-originated illusions, necessarily more or less artificial, must actually, largely create *for* us, what we imagine to be realities beyond them and independent of them. On the supposition, which I have ventured to suggest, our minds are, within the limits of their capacity, faithful and truthful media, through which is honestly conveyed to us what is presented to them.

Perhaps the question ought to have been sooner distinctly put and answered, " What are these

mysterious, essential thought-forms, these necessary mental laws, which are supposed not to report to us what is communicated to them, but actually to modify all our knowledge and to make it
specially *human*, quite different from knowledge,
possessed by other intelligent beings, at all events,
whether different or the same, or how far different
and how far the same, we can never know. What
are they? Chiefly these three—Time, Space, Personality.

I. The first, the law of Time, is *the* univeral,
the only strict universal thought-form, necessarily
affecting all the acts of consciousness, without exception. In thinking of anything, we think of it,
must think of it, as, *in time*, occupying a definite
period, preceded by something, followed by something else. Duration and succession are the two
necessary ideas. We are not taught by experience,
thus to think : it is not owing to a purpose or
choice of ours. It is involuntary, inevitable, universal, wholly *à priori*. But is there anything
here, any *new* thing, not already involved in our
nature, to cramp, to fetter, to narrow, to modify,
to alter our ideas, to make them other, than, in
any case, they *must* have been ? I maintain
there is not. The bearing of this thought-form,
on the doctrine of the Infinite, is manifest, and
the lecturer has made legitimate use of it in this relation. Within time we *cannot* condense eternity.

Within limits, we cannot compress that which has no limits. Under the mental law of time, Infinity is in-con-ceivable, in-com-prehensible. But I ask is *this*, any *new* thing, any *additional* chain, forged for us, by this peculiar thought-form ? It is simply to say, that we are created and not uncreated, that we are finite, not infinite. It is no *new* thing, but neither more nor less, than simply identical with the earlier fact involved in our creation. The finite cannot contain, com-prehend the Infinite. The *à priori* law of time is not a *new*, cramping, narrowing, modifying influence. It is simply the necessary concomitant of our created nature, and no addition to it. Above all, it is no peculiar lim-itation, belonging only to man, making his thoughts and his knowledge peculiarly human, but belonging necessarily to all created minds, be their order what it may.

II. In like manner, of the thought-form of per-sonality. We think of mental attributes, *must* think of them, *can* only think of them, as *in* an individual mind. It is possible to abstract the general quality, say, of wisdom, and to reason re-specting it, and to set it before our minds, as a separate idea. But in the same moment, in the same mental act, we necessarily localize it in a wise being. The law of personality conditions our thinking, in this sphere. Supreme intelligence, moral attributes, volitions, we are compelled to attach to a Supreme Personality.   But do we not, at the same time, most surely believe that this is the very actual fact?   Why, and on what invincible ground, shall any one assert that it is not?   Our own personality is the image and the prophecy, if not the proof of the Supreme personality.   Unless our nature be an elaborate deception, we are compelled to accept this as the very truth, involving no inconsistency, though profound mystery, which we may never be able to solve.   At all events, this can be no peculiarly *human* limitation.   Rising, necessarily, out of the very fact of personality, it must bear alike on all created minds, human and superhuman.

III. The law of Space need not be noticed.   It belongs only to one sphere, that of extended matter and of our external perceptions, and in no important sense can it be conceived to create any *new* limit for our knowledge.

The entire idea of our being cramped and fettered, by the necessary laws of thought, is unfounded and untrue.   We are creatures, finite, limited beings, and all our knowledge and our powers *are* limited.   But our Creator has not aggravated this necessary limitation, by new chains, under the name of essential thought-forms.   The conception is both more natural and more philosophical, that these, belonging to us, not peculiarly as *human,* but in common with all finite beings, are designed to help us in reaching, to the utmost extent of which our nature is capable, *the very reality* of things. It is not true that the laws of thought "impart a corresponding character to all the objects of consciousness," that is, impose on them an additional limitation of their own. It is not true that the "facts of human consciousness" are not also faithful representatives of facts in themselves. It is not true that "what is conceived under the laws of human thought" is not also actual reality. It is not true that right and wrong for man is not also right and wrong for all other intelligent beings.

CHAPTER III.

IMMUTABLE RIGHT AND WRONG.

Incapable of Judging of Divine ?—Infinite Morality ?—Absolute Morality ?—Contradictory—Bolingbroke—Regulations—Eternal Principles—No Modification—Varied Applications—Conscience —Supreme Authority.

THE work we are examining, deals with the human, only with the human ; and the human, it professes to show, is something quite by itself, peculiarly constructed and conditioned, under peculiar restrictive laws, which make all human knowledge and all human experience totally different from knowledge and experience, among other intelligent beings. Above all, it aims to separate these utterly and for ever, from all relation to the Divine Mind.

" As a corollary to this theory" (that of Kant, already referred to), " it follows that the law of human morality must be regarded as the measure and adequate representation of the moral nature of God ; in fact, that our knowledge of the Divine Being is identical with that of our own moral duties." (p. 202.) The lecturer speaks of Kant's theory as virtually maintaining " that man may become the measure of the Absolute nature of God." (p. 208.) Again, with reference to the Moral Reason, he says, " We must refuse to exalt it to the measure and standard of the Absolute and Infinite goodness of God." (p. 229.)

Perhaps it might be asked, where, even in Kant, there is just ground for this sort of inference. But, at all events, it is surely possible to maintain the authority of conscience, and the validity and reality of our moral intuitions, without exalting man to the level of his Creator, and, above all, without constituting him the measure and standard of his Creator's attributes. There are some things which even the lecturer must allow to be common to man, with the Highest Intelligence. A whole is greater than its part, parallel lines, cannot meet ; in another region the principle of gravitation reigns in the material universe, and in another region still, wisdom is better than folly. We might even venture so far as to make these, and such facts or principles, tests of any communication professing to come from above. If they were contradicted or denied, we might venture to conclude that the communication could not be divine. But should we, therefore, be chargeable with exalting *our* knowledge to the level of the *Divine*, above all, with constituting our knowledge the measure and standard of the Divine. The idea is preposterous, and as a charge, is scarcely candid or fair. But the whole drift of the lecturer is to show that human morality is one thing, divine morality (though I intensely dislike the phrase) quite another thing. " Human morality, even in its highest elevation, is not identical with, nor adequate to measure the absolute morality of God."   (p. 206.)

Taking the word absolute, in its strict philosophical meaning, the meaning belonging to it, in the earlier discussions relating to the Absolute and Infinite, that phrase, absolute morality is simply not sense, indeed, is a pure contradiction. Absolute, absolved, loosed from relation, connection, dependence, etc.   Morality is a single quality, out of many, related necessarily to other qualities, supposing their existence, essentially dependent on them ; on intelligence, for example, on perception, on volition.   If it be said it is absolute, inasmuch as it is " in and by itself," this arises from a misconception.   The Being in whom it resides is in and of Himself—that is, He is underived, self-sustained, and everlastingly self-sustaining.   But His attributes are in Him, not in and of themselves. If the word be employed popularly, to mean pure, unmixed, genuine, very morality, in its highest possible form, the sense is most true ; but the word, already preoccupied, is none the less objectionable. At all events, let us not be terrified by the grandeur of the word absolute, for here the only thing it can mean is pure, real, very.

It may be convenient, at the same time, to notice a cognate phrase, which is also repeatedly employed, *infinite morality.* I do not know what it means, or by what authority it is used. I can attach no idea to the word infinite, in this connection. Rectitude, purity, veracity, benevolence, incapable of limit, in the uncreated nature; moral excellence, the highest that can possibly exist, beyond which nothing is conceivable! To any other or more than this, I am unable to attach any idea, any meaning whatever. Infinite, in the strict philosophical sense, does convey more than this, something positive and *app*rehensible, though not *com*prehensible. The Being in whom spiritual excellence resides is strictly Infinite, because He is Eternal, unbeginning, unending, underived, unchangeable. All his perfections, physical, and moral, are in this sense strictly infinite, that they ever have been and ever shall be. But in themselves, to call them infinite, may be true, or it may be false; but to me it is wholly unintelligible. One thing is quite clear, moral attributes in the Great Being may be in exercise, or they may not be in exercise; they may be put forth in varying forms and in varying degrees. To my mind it is contradictory to predicate infinity of *that*, which admits of degrees. On the whole, these awful words Absolute morality, Infinite morality, must not be suffered to impose on us. Both are at the best unmeaning, and, at least, one is a pure contradiction.

I am not quite sure, that even the design, unconsciously, of the use of the terms we have criticized, was not to deter us from attempting to think of the moral attributes of the Creator, and to make us feel that the subject does not belong to us at all. The undoubted aim of the lecturer throughout, is to prove that moral excellence in the highest nature is altogether beyond our knowledge. Thus he says—"He from whom all holy desires, all good counsels, and all just works do proceed, must himself be more holy, more just, more good, than these. But when we try to realize in thought, this sure conviction of our faith, we find that here, as everywhere, the finite cannot fathom the infinite, that while in our hearts we believe, yet our thoughts are at times sore troubled." (p. 230.) " That there is an absolute morality, based upon, or rather identical with the eternal nature of God is indeed a conviction, forced upon us by the same evidence, as that on which we believe that God exists at all. But *what* that absolute morality is, we are as unable to fix in any human conception, as we are to define the other attributes of the same divine nature." (p. 206.) " We do not certainly know the exact nature and operation of the moral attributes of God : we can but infer and conjecture from what we know of the moral attributes of man, and the analogy between the finite and the infinite, can never be so perfect, as to preclude all possibility of error in the process." (p. 240.)

There is one writer of the last century, Lord Bolingbroke, who expresses sentiments precisely identical with those now quoted. In him they were consistent enough ; for he employed them in order to overthrow the argument for a future state. "The Divine attributes," says Bolingbroke, "are exercised in such innumerable relations, absolutely unknown to us, that though we are sure the exercise of them, in the immensity of the universe, is always directed by the all-perfect Being, to that which is fittest on the whole ; yet, the notions of created beings like us, who see them in one relation alone, cannot be applied to them, with any propriety nor with any certainty sufficient to make them objects of · our imitation." (Bol. Works, Lon. 1754, iii. 412.) Again, "as little can we rise from *our* moral obligations to God's supposed moral attributes. I call them supposed, because after all that has been said, to prove a necessary connection between his physical, and his moral attributes, the latter may all be absorbed in his wisdom." (iv. 18.) "God is in their (theologians') notion of him, nothing more than an Infinite man. He knows as we know, is wise as we are wise, and moral as we are moral." (iv. 296.) "Clarke's whole chain of reasoning, from the moral attributes downwards, is nothing more than one continued application of *human moral ideas* to the design and conduct of God." (v. 5.) "It required no such metaphysical apparatus, as he (Sam. Clarke) employed, somewhat tediously, to prove that all perfections, physical and moral, must be attributes of the self-existent, all-perfect author of all being ; but he does not prove what he asserts, and on the proof of which his whole argument turns, that these attributes are the same in God, as they are in our ideas." (iv. 249.)

These sound to me like extracts from the Bampton Lecture ; they contain the very ideas put forth in it ; but they are the words of Lord Bolingbroke. None could be more earnest than he was, in his day, to prove that the moral attributes of the Great Being are unknown, and unknowable by man.

There is one distinction between the Divine and the human, in which a source of difficulty is found, which it is not easy to appreciate. " To human conception, it seems impossible that absolute morality should be manifested in the form of a law of obligation, for such a law implies relation and subjection to the authority of a lawgiver. All human morality is manifested in this form." (p. 206.) I humbly conceive, that all the difficulty here represented, vanishes with a simple statement of the accepted facts. There is a law within the human mind, commanding right, forbidding wrong. There is also an inward sense of obligation to obey that law. It is in *this* way that human morality is manifested. On the other hand, the Supreme always is and does that which is immutably right. It is his essential nature, to be and do that which is immutably right. He would not be God, He would cease to be, were it otherwise. There are no lawgiver and no law to Him, no obedience, no sense of obligation ; but only the silent evolution of an eternal fact, the serene energy of a changeless nature. What is law to us, is life to the Supreme ; what is obligation to us, is mere being to Him. And what then ? Where is the difficulty ?

The real question at issue is not touched at all— " Is there, or is there not, that which is immutably right, that which is immutably wrong—the same to all created minds, and to the uncreated ? Have we, or have we not, the power of distinguishing that which is immutably right and that which is immutably wrong ? Is rectitude rectitude, uprightness uprightness, dishonesty dishonesty, generosity generosity, malignity malignity, deceit deceit, to us and to all beings, and to the Great God ?" The question is intelligible, direct, simple. I put it in the shortest form, Is a lie a lie, all the universe over, in all places and at all times, and amongst all rational and moral beings ? There may be doubt whether a thing be true or false, or how far it is the one or the other. There may be doubt whether the utterer or the doer of it were aware of its falsity, or how far he was aware of it. But suppose the thing to be a palpable, naked falsehood, is it, or is it not, a falsehood all the universe over ; is it, or is it not, eternally, immutably wrong, a thing to be only scouted, scorned, hated, reprobated ? Can we conceive a single sane mind, of God's creating, of any order, in any part of space, thinking it other than eternally, immutably wrong ? Phenomenon of consciousness ? It *is* phenomenon. But there is reality behind it, and it is *this*, of which we take hold, and know that we take hold. It is such a phenomenon, so actual, so real, that it scorches, and scars, and damns the mind in which it is begotten. It is, and we know that it *is*, an actual, execrable, burning abomination, in God's universe. We *do*, in our measure, know some things, this among others, *in themselves*, as they really are, and as they are judged by all creatures, and by the Creator !

Our impressions of evil, as of everything else, depend on our mental capacity, and on the amount of our intelligence. A powerful, instructed, disciplined mind, will see falsehood as another cannot. But to both, with stronger or feebler impressions, it is *essentially* the same—a thing, only and immutably wrong.

The Bampton lecturer, if I rightly understand

him, would have us abandon all investigation into fixed moral principles, and would substitute for them certain ascertained rules of life. As in the intellectual, so here also in the moral region, his conviction seems to be that the moment we pass from the world of the senses to the world of thought, from practical to speculative truth, we insure nothing but perplexity. Take, as an example, the following on the subject of principles— "To maintain the immutability of moral principles in the abstract, is a very different thing from maintaining the immutability of the particular acts by which those principles are manifested in practice. That duty ought, in all cases, to be followed, in preference to inclination, is as certain a truth as that two straight lines cannot inclose a space. In their concrete application, both principles are equally liable to error. . . . . It is in their concrete form that moral principles are adopted as guides of conduct and canons of judgment, and in this form they admit of various degrees of uncertainty or of positive error." (p. 207.) Poor guides they must be! useless canons! one would think, if this be true. There are cases of casuistry, Protestant as well as Roman Catholic, which fill many goodly volumes. And if the great principles of morality depended, as the lecturer seems to think they do, on the solution of such cases, we may as well, at once, throw ourselves at

the feet of divines, of either school, or both ; for
no training of ordinary men could possibly fit
them for such a task. But what shall we think
of the elevation to the dignity of a moral principle, of the statement, " that duty ought always to
be followed in preference to inclination." Moral
principle ? it is no moral principle. It is a sound
maxim, a judgment which most men have arrived
at. But moral principles are given in a shorter,
simpler, terser, sterner form. Be just, be truthful, be upright and sincere, be loving and generous ! Duty ! the word is short enough, but it is
made, in experience, endlessly complex and com-
plicated. There are many real and many more
unreal difficulties, connected with the determination of what in modern phrases is called duty. It
touches a thousand things, more or less related or
conflicting, which are made to encumber the simple moral imperative, the *ought* and *ought not*.
We think of interests, immediately personal or
relative, of social obligations and influences, of actual surrounding conditions, of results and effects,
of public opinion, of pleasure or pain, to others of
inclination or bias, for or against. But the question
is far shorter, easier, simpler, " shall I utter or act
a falsehood ? shall I be guilty of clear injustice ?
shall I practise a deception ? shall I perpetrate a
cruelty ?" These are questions which in 999 cases

out of every 1,000, even a child knows to answer, in a moment.

The lecturer keeps far away from the great, immutable principles of right or wrong. Apparently, human morality is to him something doubtful, fluctuating, and changeable. He, in fact, speaks of " moral obligation, conceived as a law binding on man, to be regarded as immutable, so *long as man's nature remains unchanged.*" (p. 204.) Again, of " morality in its human character, depending *on conditions not co-eternal* with God." (p. 210.) It would not be equitable, were I to omit to say, that in these, and such cases, he has reference to what are called *positive* commands of God touching things indifferent in themselves, but binding, because they are commanded. As most forcibly illustrating the principle involved, I take the fact that the Jews, by command of God, gave a tenth of their property to their religion, that a particular tribe were priests by birth, wore certain robes, and performed certain ceremonies at certain times, and in a prescribed mode. These things were neither right nor wrong in themselves, human conscience had nothing to do with them, save in one point ; they were to the Jews express commands of their God. And reason and conscience witness to this as a first principle, " God is to be obeyed unreservedly." We may be right or we may be wrong in construing his voice, but that voice recognized, obe-

dience is imperative. Here is *the one* moral principle, in all that can be regarded as circumstantial
and positive, in human duty—implicit obedience
to God. But *this* has nothing circumstantial,
local, temporary, fluctuating in it; it is eternal,
immutable, universal, a law not to man only, but
to all created natures. *This* stands on the same
basis with eternal justice, veracity, sincerity, and
benevolence.

But the aim of the lecturer is not to identify
human morality with everlasting principles, but to
reduce it to what is merely positive and locally or
temporarily regulative. He speaks of the great
principles of all that is holy and righteous existing
in God, before they assumed *their finite form* in
the heart of man." (p. 210.) What is the finite in
distinction from any other form of rectitude, veracity, uprightness and benevolence? I do not
know. Again, " God did not create absolute morality, it is co-eternal with himself, and it were
blasphemy to say that there ever was a time when
God was and Goodness was not. But God did
create the human manifestation of morality," (p.
208), that is to say, he did create a human manifestation of that which was in Himself and was
uncreated. We must understand this, as the undoubted import of the structure of the sentence.
The eternal principles of right and wrong are un-
created, but a human manifestation of them *was*

created. *That* must mean, I imagine, a human medium for manifesting them was created. The lecturer adds, God did create *this* manifestation, " when he created the moral constitution of man." Of course he did. The moral constitution of man was the new medium, through which eternal moral principles were manifested. No, by no means, this is not what the lecturer would say, for he adds, God did create the human manifestation of morality, " when he placed man in those circumstances, by which the eternal principles of right and wrong *are modified* in relation to this present life." *This* is not manifestation, it is not the mere application of principles to certain new circumstances, but *modification.*

To modify, is to alter, so as to suit circumstances. We modify a statement, when we find, either that it contained too much or did not contain enough, to be strictly true. We modify a scheme, when, finding either that it will not work, or not so efficiently as we anticipated, we correct its provisions, or introduce new ones. We modify a principle, when experience has taught us that in one direction and another, it is not really sound, or is defective. To modify is to alter. And the eternal principles of right and wrong are not merely *applied* to this present life, but *altered,* how far we know not, but they are so far altered that from human morality, we cannot judge *what*

real, essential morality is, or may be. If this be
not to shake the everlasting foundations of the
moral universe, what can be? No wonder then
the lecturer should say, " while in our hearts
we believe, yet our thoughts at times are sore
troubled." No wonder then he should find
" many things, impossible to understand and difficult to believe." And his hitherto strong refuge,
Butler, whose chief glory, it appears to me, no
one has labored more effectually—though without
such an intention—than he, to cast in the dust ;
his chosen refuge cannot avail him here. True
enough, " the very philosopher whose writings
have most contributed to establish the supreme
authority of conscience in man, is also the one,
who has pointed out most clearly the existence of
analogous moral difficulties in nature and in religion, and the true answer to both, namely the admission, that God's government, natural as well as
spiritual, is a scheme, *imperfectly comprehended.*"
(p. 229.)

All or nearly all will admit that God's government *is* imperfectly comprehended. But what of
the modification, the alteration of the eternal principles of right and wrong, *in relation to this present life?* What of human morality as a different
thing from real, genuine, essential morality?
This is no imperfect comprehension of God's
government, it is comprehending, only too clearly,

the unstable and flexible character of moral law. Butler maintains nothing like this, he does not, in the most indirect way, hint at such a thing. The very contrary. Butler upholds the doctrine of conscience as a power in the soul, percipient of immutable right and wrong, an authority commanding the one, forbidding the other. Referring to disputed commands in the Old Testament, he says, "none of these precepts," (in the very passage quoted by Mr. Mansell, p. 243,) "*are contrary to immutable morality.*" Immutable morality! *He* holds that we can know it and judge what is and what is not contrary to it. The Bampton lecturer could not have employed the phrase, for he distinctly maintains that we *cannot* know it.— There is, he might have said, an immutable morality, but what it is, we are wholly unable to fix in any human conception. Not so, Butler. So clear, and sure, and fixed is our conception of it, in his opinion, that he puts it against a conceived, not actual, statement in the scriptures, and asserts its supremacy. "*If* it were commanded," he says, "to cultivate the principles and to act in the spirit of treachery, ingratitude, cruelty, the command,"—in the bible he means—even a command in the bible—"would not alter the nature of the case or of the action, in any of these instances. But it is quite otherwise in precepts which require only the doing an external action." (p. 243.)

There can be no interpretation, but one, of this passage. Conscience, in the sphere of the highest moral principles, is the ultimate authority, from which there is no appeal. Everywhere, for all beings, and for ever and ever, these principles are immoveable. The law of the inward judge is paramount. Nothing can compete with it. Butler shall tell us, that not even a command in the bible—were such a thing possible—not even a command in the bible, however seemingly express and plain, could alter the case. There is nothing here, of the modification of eternal right and wrong; nothing here of distinguishing human morality, from eternal, essential morality.

To those who, with myself, bow to the authority of the holy scriptures, there may be a nobler and fuller revelation of moral life, than can be reached, in the absence of such divine aid, and a clearer and more extended interpretation of moral law. But where there are no scriptures, thank God! there is a conscience, a voice from above, within man, testifying to the highest and grandest truth. Take this away! as in effect and in fact, the Bampton lecturer does, and the divinest light that yet lingers in the human soul is put out. Reduce morals to a calculation of probabilities, a science of ecclesiastical casuistry, let virtue depend on a weighing and balancing of advantages, personal and relative, on a measuring of effects, near and remote, on each man's sagacity and honesty and temper in judging, let there be no innate sense of right and wrong, no ultimate authoritative judge, let eternal justice, veracity and uprightness, witnessed by conscience, be banished from language, as amiable but imbecile mistakes, and the very foundations of the moral universe are upturned and the reign of a hopeless, eternal, moral anarchy is inaugurated.

The imperfections and even perversions of natural conscience are undeniable. Like the bodily senses and the powers of the mind, *this*, also admits of being improved and impaired. But it remains notwithstanding, as they also do ; it remains an imperishable part of our constitution, precious above all others, as the source of immutable, moral intuitions. "It is not," says Dr. Chalmers, meeting the case of contradictory, ethical conclusions in different countries and ages, " it is not that Justice, Humanity, and Gratitude are not the canonized virtues of every region, or that Falsehood, Cruelty, and Fraud would not, in their abstract and unassociated nakedness, be viewed as the objects of moral antipathy and rebuke. . . . In spite of all the topical moralities, to which various causes have given birth, there is an unquestioned universal morality notwithstanding. And in every case, where the moral sense is unfettered by these associations and the judgment is uncramped either by the partialities of interest or by the inveteracy of national customs, which habit and antiquity have rendered sacred, . . . conscience is found to speak the same language ; nor to the remotest ends of the world, is there a country or an island where the same uniform and consistent voice is not heard from her."—*Moral and Intellectual Constitution of Man*, I. 89–91.

If the conclusions which have been successively arrived at, in the progress of this criticism, be valid, the following is something like the result :—The Bampton lecturer has dethroned human reason, has reduced all truth to a mode of our conceptions, has put out the lamp of revelation, denying that the true God, *as He is*, is to be found there, and has thus left the outer temple void and dark. But in his reasonings on our moral nature, he has done something yet more to be lamented. He has put forth his hand to the very altar of the innermost sanctuary of our being, has extinguished the sacred fire on that altar, and has written on the whole structure—Ichabod, the glory is departed ! I venture to lift a humble, feeble voice against this sacrilege. For one, I must stand, at all hazards, by what I regard as among the clearest and surest utterances of consciousness, the existence of a moral sense ! For one, I must abide, as on the very essential ground of the moral universe, by immutable morality, revealed by conscience and common to all intelligent beings. So much the more absolutely must I cling to these, because, on the principles of the Bampton lecturer, I can see nothing for man but darkness — darkness above, below, around, everywhere ; darkness in this world, darkness hereafter, darkness for ever and ever ; dreary, hopeless, overwhelming darkness ; an eternal, intolerable agony of darkness !

Only in a passing sentence or two, shall I notice the peculiar method in which the lecturer defends the mysteries of Christianity, the doctrines of the Trinity, the Incarnation, the Atonement. It is well known that objectors against these doctrines have been wont to assert that they are not only incomprehensible, but directly contradictory. The answer of the lecturer amounts to a free admission of all the alleged contradictions. It is even so, he would say, but the objection has no validity as applied to the Christian revelation, for it is only common to it, with all philosophy and with all the efforts of reason, when directed to the nature of God, or to his procedure with his creatures, or to his purposes and methods. We cannot reason upon them without being plunged into contradictions without end. We have no right to reason upon them all. They belong to the region of faith—they are to be accepted unconditionally. The Infinite and all that relates to the Infinite is not an object of human thought. We have no business to think, we are utterly incapable of conceiving anything at all on the subject.

It occurs to me, that there are others besides Christians who might make very admirable use of this mode of silencing objections. There is a doctrine, very venerable by antiquity, and as having been devoutly held, as being held at this moment by myriads of the human race—the doctrine of *The All*—no individual, personal God, but *The All*—one immanent life, for ever and ever developing itself and absorbing back into itself what it gives forth, an everlasting egress and regress, outcoming and resumption. All alleged contradictions, its adherents might maintain, have no validity. The subject does not belong to the sphere of human thought at all. It is inconceivable, and therefore the moment reason approaches it, it *can* find in it nothing but contradictions. This high, transcendental method of dismissing objections would lead, logically, to some curious results. No Protestant, for example, could utter a word against such a dogma as transubstantiation, to name no other. The ultra Calvinists, also, to whom the lecturer seems to bear little love, and their doctrine of eternal justification and eternal reprobation, would be perfectly safe. They have only to utter

the magical words—" The Infinite is not an object
of human thought at all—this belongs to the region
of the unconditioned, into which you have no right
to enter." With these words, all difficulty vanishes and victory is complete.

It is little likely, that accomplished and earnest
theologians, in our own or any other country, will
be found willing to accept of this kind of shelter
for doctrines, which they hold dear. Time was,
when the battle of the faith was fought on other
and far nobler ground, and erudite and able men
contended, triumphantly contended, that that
which they admitted to be altogether incomprehensible, could not be shown to be contradictory.
That time, one may piously hope, is not yet past.
Meanwhile, so far as the Bampton lecturer is concerned, those who have separated themselves from
Christianity, are completely triumphant, and have
had conceded to them all that they ever contended
for. They have always alleged, they do now allege,
that Christianity has no foundation in reason, cannot stand on the ground of reason. The lecturer
simply acknowledges the fact. In his view, Christianity is *as* full of *as* insoluble contradictions, as
he imagines philosophy to be. But it does not
seem to occur to him, that in such a case, wisdom
would teach us, not to adopt the one, because it is
no worse than the other, but to reject both, for the
same reason.

I see an alternative, one, only one—either to yield unconditionally to authority and throw ourselves into the arms of an infallible church, or in blank despair, to enshroud and entomb ourselves amidst all the horrors of a universal scepticism.

SECTION SIXTH.

CONCERNING REASON AND FAITH.

CONCERNING REASON AND FAITH.

THERE are two words, Reason and Faith, occurring, especially the first of the two, I know not how often, in the Bampton Lecture. Neither of them is once defined, or, in any precise manner, explained. I have attempted to show that the lecturer, in his use of the term, reason, means simply the understanding, the faculty of judgment, the power which discriminates, reasons, infers, deduces and judges. The doctrine of Leibnitz, Kant, though as announced by him, there is much confusion and inaccuracy, Cousin, Coleridge, Hamilton, and the modern philosophy of Europe, with the exception of one or two eminent English names, is that there exists a higher reason in man—intellect proper, the source of intuitive *a priori* truths. Farther still, there is a moral sense, what Kant desigates, the practical reason—the source of moral intuitions. Our English name is conscience, a power percipient of right and wrong, an authority commanding the one, forbidding the other. These three—omitting the popular use of the word as synonymous with general, human intelligence—the understanding, the intellect, the conscience, include all the strictly legitimate applications of the term, reason.

Faith, so far as it belongs to philosophy, has two distinct, but closely related senses, into one or other of which all its applications may be resolved. First of all, it is simply equivalent to belief, holding for true and real. Secondly, it is used to mean confidence, trust in a statement, a principle, a person, in anything. The second of these senses, necessarily, includes the first, but the first may exist without the second. We may firmly believe a thing to be true, in which there may be no need, not even a possibility, for the exercise of trust or confidence. But that in which we confide, we must, first of all, necessarily, hold to be true. Confidence is often only belief intensified, the same thing but in a more emphatic form. At the same time, there is a real, generic difference between the two. Simple belief is purely intellectual, confidence is always partly moral, an act not of the understanding merely, but still more of the heart, perhaps also of the conscience. The inward nature *takes hold* of that which it believes, *commits* itself to it, as true, and *rests* in it.

But whether in the sense of trust, or in that of simple belief, the question is, what is the exact relation between faith and reason—the lower, the higher or the moral reason ? Within certain limits, the answer to this question can create no difficulty. Belief, in the usual meaning of the word, belief grounded in the conclusions of the understanding, is perfectly intelligible and explicable. Through the ordinary mental processes, we inquire, examine and make ourselves acquainted with the subject, thoroughly understand it, and admit and adopt what commends itself to our minds, as true. In the same way, we receive from others a statement of facts, the testimony appears to us sufficient, and satisfactory, and we credit it. In all this we act clearly and solely on the ground of the understanding—the measure of our knowledge is the measure of our faith.

It is quite true, that so soon as a thing commends itself to our minds, so soon as we thoroughly understand it and find its evidence sufficient, we *must* believe it. It may be distasteful. We may *wish* not to believe it, we may *assert* that we *do not* believe it, but we *must*, nevertheless ; we *do*, in point of fact. Seeing a thing to be true, and believing it are identical. But it is sufficiently palpable, that the apparent necessity in this case is owing, in great part, to ourselves, is self-created. It is *we*, who according to our inclination, look or refuse to look at truth, *we* who examine or refuse to examine evidence, *we* who suffer prejudice, in one direction or another, to sway our minds or who resist the force of prejudice. At last, belief is *our* deliberate *act*, grounded in the perceptions and conclusions of our understanding. Knowledge is the basis and the measure of the act. We believe, because we understand, and so far as we understand and no farther.

All the difficulty in determining the exact relation between reason and faith, lies in quite another region. Before touching this, however, I must notice some distinctions, often overlooked, but which have a very essential bearing on the subject.

The act of consciousness is altogether involuntary and necessary. I cannot avoid being conscious of what is passing in my mind. It does not depend on my will. I *am* conscious, whether I will or no. For this reason, consciousness is its own ground, and needs and can have no other. I *know*, that I know, that I feel, that I will, that this thought is in my mind at this moment. I *know* it. You cannot go beyond this. You can get no proof whatever of the fact from any other quarter, nothing, except this immediate necessary knowledge. Consciousness wants no proof, it has no ground beyond itself. It is its own ground.

External perception also is necessary and involuntary. With my eyes open, I cannot avoid perceiving, whether I will or no. I see that tree, that book, that flower. It cannot be proved by any other evidence. I see it, that is all, I know that I see it. You cannot go farther, it is its own ground. The intuitions of the higher reason and of the conscience, belong to the same category. "The soul, God, immortality, immutable right and wrong—these and other such are data of reason and conscience. The understanding may consent to them as true, may be able to find strong confirmations of their truth. But they are not discovered by the understanding, they are not arrived at by reasoning, and they may not be capable of being logically demonstrated. They are first of all given in consciousness, they are utterances of the soul from within to itself, internal readings, intellections, announcements by the reason and conscience, and in common with the intuitions of sense, and with all the acts of consciousness, they are simply their own ground.

Faith, whether in the sense of belief, or in that of confidence, belongs to quite another order of powers. It is essentially secondary, that is, it supposes something prior to itself, on which it rests. Unlike consciousness, perception, and reason, it is not necessary but dependent, generally all but universally dependent, on our will. It does not arise out of our mental constitution, whether we will or no, but is a capacity, which we may or may not exercise, according to our inclination or our purpose. Hence it is essentially connected with responsibility—it is a virtue, and its opposite may be a crime. Consciousness, perception, and the intuitions of reason, are neither right nor wrong, on our part, neither wise nor unwise. To be conscious, is no merit and no fault, neither to be praised nor to be blamed. It is the mere necessary act of our nature, with which we have nothing to do, except to acknowledge it. But is faith, thus indifferent, either intellectually or morally ? On the contrary, it cannot be doubted for a moment, that faith may be, *must* be, always, either right or wrong, wise or unwise. Its character is determined by the grounds on which it is based.

One additional distinction remains, belief or faith is in no respect creative, not even perceptive, but only and wholly re-ceptive. It is not an organ for discovering truth, or even for *per*-ceiving truth that had otherwise been unseen. It supposes something presented to it, something already discovered and perceived by another organ, and its entire office is to hold it for true, and to admit and adopt it. It does not supply its own materials, but simply acts on materials presented to it. We believe. The first question is, in what?—something presented to us, through another medium. The second question is, on what grounds? and are the grounds valid or invalid? These questions—questions belonging altogether to the understanding—can be determined in no other way than every other act of our rational nature is determined. The mere *fact* of consciousness, without asking a single question, is sufficient, we are entitled to take our stand upon it, itself alone. *If* I am *conscious* of a certain thought, feeling, state of mind, at this moment, it *cannot* be gainsaid. Nothing can be surer. But the mere act of faith is of no value at all. It depends entirely on the grounds on which it is based —whether they be wise and valid, or the contrary. It would be pure fanaticism, utter irrationality, capable of every sort of abuse, to say, "I believe this or that, I can give no ground for it, but I firmly believe it." In no respect, can the mere act of faith be either its own evidence or its own ground. Invariably, the question must abide—a question, altogether, of the understanding—believe in what? on what grounds?

The great difficulty—real or imagined—is in the application of the principles now laid down to what are called "primary beliefs," the reality of which I, for one, most fully and cordially recognize. There are, it is maintained, beliefs or trusts, native to the soul, immediate, irresistible, ultimate facts, beyond which we cannot go. In loose, current phrase there are intuitions of sense and intuitions of reason, including both our purely intellectual and our moral intuitions. I am fully prepared to grant, in opposition to the idealist, that we do put faith, and are justified in putting faith, in our sense-perceptions ; and in opposition to a mere sensational, materialistic, positive philosophy, that we do put faith, and are justified in putting faith, in the intuitions of reason and conscience and in consciousness, in which alone, both the higher and the lower intuitions are given. I hold that we are so constituted, as to entertain these primary beliefs, and that in spite of seeming exceptions, they are immediate, and all but irresistible. But I deny altogether, that either the character or the law of faith is hereby, in any respect, altered. It is still secondary, dependent and purely *receptive*. Instead of being its own ground, it is grounded—as the mere statement of the psychological facts shows—in perception, or in reason, or in conscience, and throughout in consciousness. Instead of being arbitrary and unaccountable, instead of being opposed to the higher reason, instead of being even independent of it, faith, as it respects our primary beliefs, is consciously sanctioned, nay demanded by the reason, as a necessary act of obedience. Faith, in the cases alluded to, true faith, is *itself* the highest reason, is simply obedience to

the highest reason — the consummation and the
crown of our intellectual activity.

There is even more. Our primary beliefs, in the
farthest analysis, are capable of being resolved into
an indestructible conclusion of the understanding.
The deep, inward ultimate ground, understood and
felt by multitudes who cannot express it, in definite words, is no other than this—our perceptions,
our intuitions, our consciousnesses *must* be true, *because otherwise our nature is a falsehood and our
Creator a deceiver.* This is the last strong refuge
of faith in these primary convictions. We could
believe nothing, if *they* were not to be believed.
All within us and all around us, everywhere, would
be only delusion and mockery. And thus the
highest faith *is* resolved into a simple judgement,
an act of the calm, sober understanding.

But some of the truths of intuition are altogether incomprehensible, and, at least, *this* seems
not consistent with the law of faith as already
expounded. The Unbeginning, Unending, Un-
changing One is incomprehensible. Infinite duration is incomprehensible, utterly incomprehensible.
But, it must be remembered that all these are data
of the higher reason, or rather, as I venture to
think, inferences of the understanding from data
of the reason. Faith has thus not only reason to
sustain it, but a double ground in the understanding and the reason, and, therefore, legitimately

takes hold of, *apprehends* that which nevertheless cannot be *com*-prehended in thought. Even the Bampton lecturer, *in words*, sustains this issue. "Reason itself," he says, "rightly interpreted, *teaches* the existence of truths that are above reason"—that is, which are imcomprehensible. And again, "It is a duty *enjoined* by reason itself to believe in that which we are unable to comprehend." Quite so ; and, therefore, faith is manifestly based on reason. We may judge with what consistency, and in connection with the words now quoted, the lecturer can assert, "We thus learn that the provinces of reason and faith are not co-extensive." (p. 96.) But if, as he had just maintained, reason enjoins what faith obeys, and as in the first quotation, if reason teaches what faith adopts, it is shown, so far at least, that their provinces *are* co-extensive.

I turn to the language of Sir William Hamilton on this point, beautifully *exact* and true to the letter. "We are thus taught," he says, " the salutary lesson, that *the capacity of thought* is not to be constituted into the *measure of existence*, and are warned from recognizing the domain of our *knowledge* (that is our com-prehension) as necessarily co-extensive with the horizon of our faith." He never opposes *reason* to faith, never opposes even *knowledge* to faith ; but only maintains that the one extends beyond the other. The Bampton lecturer, on the contrary, speaks of "The conflicting claims of reason and faith."

After describing the contradictions that arise out of the idea of the Infinite or Absolute, he adds, "This tells with equal force against all belief and all unbelief, and therefore, necessitates the conclusion that belief *cannot* be determined *solely* by reason." (p. 59.) Belief is not always determined by *reasoning*, not always by *knowledge i. e.* com-pre-hen-sion ; sometimes it has its ground in intuition. But I have tried to show that *in all cases* it must be determined, either by the higher or by the lower reason, or by both. By what else *can* it be determined ? There is no single power within us and no combination of powers apart from the understanding and the intellect, through which belief can be produced. Again, "In this impotence of reason, we are compelled to take refuge in faith, and to believe that an Infinite Being exists, though we know not how." (p. 120.)

It is reason which impels or compels us to believe that an Infinite Being exists. Instead of fleeing from the one to take refuge in the other, it is reason which in this case teaches what faith adopts—reason which enjoins what faith obeys. Instead of being uncongenial and irreconcilable, the two are in perfect harmony, faith all the while leaning on reason for support. One other passage will suffice. "In thus believing we desert the evidence of reason to rest on that of faith and of the principles on which reason itself depends, it is obviously impossible to have any other guarantee."—(p. 146.) We *may*, in many instances, have to transcend the evidence furnished by the *understanding* merely. That may be insufficient. But to desert even this for the evidence of faith, is to abandon that which *is* something, however inadequate, for that which is literally nothing. By no possibility can our mere faith in anything furnish the least evidence that the thing is true and real ; and as for being a guarantee, and the only guarantee, of the principles on which reason itself depends, if there be force in what has been already advanced, this must at once be seen to be the very opposite of the truth.

Graphically and beautifully, faith is said by an inspired penman, to *substantiate* things hoped for ; that is, by its all-absorbing force, to give them, to our sensibilities, the solidity of a real presence. Graphically and beautifully, it is said, to *e-vidence* things not seen,—that is, to bring them out into clear light, and to present them before our eyes. But *evidence*, meaning *proof* of its objects, in any possible, intelligible sense, it can furnish none. The mere act of believing or confiding in anything, in itself, is of no value at all. All the value that can belong to it depends entirely on the grounds on which it is based. Faith merely takes hold of that which *has* been seen to be true, which, *previously and on other grounds* has been seen to be true. It is supposed that, first of all, we find a thing to be true and trustworthy; whether it be so or not, actually, is still a question, but the evidence, at least, has satisfied us, and on the ground of this we put faith in it. Indisputably, the faith cannot be the proof of its truth.

It must be acknowledged that Hamilton, in his notes on Reid, employs language which goes far, too far, to support that of the Bampton Lecture. Two things, however, are to be noted : first, that *he* does not refer to faith in its usual and general meaning, but only to a certain limited class of beliefs, those called primary, native, intuitive ; secondly, even these primary beliefs he does not place in opposition to reason, but only holds that their ground, and the ground of reason itself, lie in something which he conceives to be beyond reason.

" Reason itself," says he, " must rest at last upon authority, for the original data of reason do not rest on reason; but are necessarily accepted by reason, on the authority of what is beyond itself." —(*Hamilton's Reid*, p. 760.) What authority, we may ask, especially ask Hamilton, is there or can there be *within us*, superior to the higher reason ? None. There is no power in our nature superior or even equal to this. And if the authority referred to be an authority, *ab extra*, *that*, first, can only be reached by us ; secondly, can only reach us through our reason, intellectual or moral—as a datum of this highest power ; so that reason, even in such a case, is and must be the ultimate ground on which faith rests. And, besides, who is entitled to assert that the data of reason *cannot* rest on reason ? Do not the data of consciousness rest on consciousness, on consciousness alone ? I am conscious of this or that thought in my mind. Where is the proof ? I know it. I can have no other proof ; I want no other. I know it as a fact within me ; it is enough. So, also, I am distinctly aware of this or that intuition. I see it, I read it, as written and laid up in the *locus principiarum;* my higher reason announces it as true. If it be suggested, as it may legitimately be suggested, that in both of these instances we *can*, in addition to their own proper ground, and *do* fall back on our nature and on the great Being who created it. It is granted. The authority of our Creator is paramount. He is to be implicitly believed and trusted. But there is a reason for this. It is because even the understanding teaches that we could believe nothing, unless we believed this. In other words, we come back to the very ground of rationality. *The* principle which we adopt in this case is one which the understanding and the intellect not only sanction but demand. This faith is faith altogether grounded in reason.

" In the last resort," Hamilton adds, " we must, perforce, philosophically admit that belief is the primary condition of reason, not reason the ultimate ground of belief." (p. 760.) By no means ; for, when we accept the data of reason, it is because we have ground in our nature and in Him who created it for believing that these data are true, because we are satisfied that the reason which furnishes these data legitimately deserves our faith. Again, Hamilton adds : " We are compelled to surrender the proud *intellige ut credas* of Abelard, to content ourselves with the humble *crede ut intelligas* of Anselm." (p. 760.) But why may not both maxims be profoundly and equally true ? I hold that they are. We should err egregiously by adopting the first alone, but not less egregiously should we err by adopting the second alone. Both together must be taken in order to reach the whole truth. Examine, search patiently, get to understand and know, in order that you may enlightenedly adopt. On the other hand, accept what the higher reason announces, in order that you may ponder it, penetrate it, and understand it as far as it can be understood. It is even possible to put Anselm's maxim in a higher and more modest form still, than he gave it, *crede, etiamsi non intelligas— etiamsi nunquam intellecturus sis.* Some of the data of reason are incomprehensible by the understanding. But they are **true**; the ground of the reason whereon they stand is sufficient basis for them to rest upon, though to their full and grand compass of meaning we shall never be able to reach.

The general results at which we have arrived are these. First of all, we put faith in the conclusions of the understanding ; and these, of course, may be right or they may be wrong. But we believe that which we think we understand and because we understand it, and only so far as we understand it, our knowledge being both the basis and the measure of our faith. Secondly, we put faith in the intuitions, first, of sense, and second of reason, intellectual and moral. And lastly, we put faith in consciousness, the witness alike of our intuitions and of all our acts of knowledge. Throughout, in all cases, the ground of faith is either the understanding, or the higher reason, or both. Our mere faith itself determines nothing, proves nothing. Its worth or worthlessness depends entirely on the character of its grounds. Universally, the question must be put, Are these grounds wise, right, sufficient ? in one word, are they rational.

There remains one possible source, which the Bampton lecturer seems to have had chiefly in his thought, whence the materials of belief or faith may be de-riv-ed. That source is written revelation. With many of the questions here arising, most of which belong exclusively to the understanding, the logical understanding, the faculty of judgment, we have nothing to do. For example, by what external marks, seals and proofs, that which claims to be from heaven, evinces itself indisputably to be so, is not a question for us. So also, by what canons of criticism, what principles and modes of interpretation, we are to be guided in dealing with what is written, so as most surely to reach its true meaning and to determine the sense of disputed texts, are not questions for us. By the way, only by the way, there is one canon, to which, inasmuch as it is perfectly general and has a peculiar recommendation, I may give prominence. If we attach weight to the authority of Butler, we shall ponder his deliberately expressed verdict, already quoted : "None of these precepts "—disputed precepts in the Old Testament—"are contrary to immutable morality. If it were commanded to cultivate the principles and act in the spirit of treachery, ingratitude, cruelty, the command would not alter the nature of the case or of the action, in any of these instances." I say, we shall ponder his words and shall learn from him to lay it down as one of the fixed laws of interpretation, that that cannot be divine, which is in the face of the immutable principles of reason and conscience. Should any sacred text seem to contradict these principles, we *may* doubt our interpretation of the text, we may, we *must* dismiss that interpretation as certainly false, but we *may not*, must not for a moment suffer the faintest suspicion of these principles to darken our minds. Revelation may make known that which neither unaided reason nor conscience has ever uttered. Revelation may announce that which is far beyond and above all intimations from within, may announce even that which transcends the comprehension of the finite mind. But what is in manifest contradiction to the immutable principles of morality, revelation *never* can promulgate, for this would be to make the Great Being contradict himself. All this, by the way. Such matters do not fall within our proper sphere.

What we have to suppose is this, the conviction lodged in a human mind that certain words express a real message from the Almighty, and that the message conveys such or such a distinct meaning ; the result is a firm belief in *this* meaning, as the very thought of the Supreme. What is the nature of this belief or faith and on what is it grounded ? In reference to the preliminary stages which lead to this final result, there is no room for difference of opinion. For example, manifestly, it may be true or it may be false, that there *is* a *divine* voice in certain words. We may have come to a right or to a wrong conclusion on this point. It is certainly one which *can* be ascertained only through the processes of the understanding, or through the intuitions of reason, or through both. In like manner it may be true or it may be false, that *the* meaning which *we* have attached to the Divine voice is the correct one. We may have come to a right or to a wrong conclusion on this point. It is certainly one which *can* be ascertained only in the exercise of the common faculty of judgment. Thus far the act of our minds is manifestly grounded in reason. But does the faith which we repose in the ideas which we have thus reached, demand quite a new exposition. It is faith no longer in man, no longer in ourselves, no longer in reason, but in the immediate word of the Supreme. Be it so. Certainly, the mental act does terminate in the Great Being, as its object, and *there* reposes with confidence. But why? Unaccountably? arbitrarily? in a way of which no explanation can be given? No. But because, simply and only because the understanding, the intellect and the conscience unite in announcing it as their imperative demand, that, of all things, *He* is to be believed. Here and everywhere, true faith is grounded in reason. It *can* be grounded in nothing else.

It is possible, legitimately to extend the idea of supernatural communication, beyond the limits of the sacred text. Philosophy at least has nothing to object against this extension. The daemon of Socrates contains the germ of an imperishable

truth. There is a widely extended belief in the
direct intercourse—altogether mysterious and incomprehensible as it is—of the Infinite with the
finite mind. The idea is inexpressibly healing and
strengthening, that the great speaker, unheard by
the outward ear ; and the great worker, unseen by
the outward eye—the speaker to minds, the worker
in minds—ceaseless, universal, impartial in his influence, is the Creator and Father of men. Where
a human mind is found, His secret voice is never
silent, *His* invisible energy is never at rest. It
appears to be in harmony with the soundest philosophy to believe that the unspoken word of the
Eternal is heard—might be heard far oftener than
it is—within the individual soul.

But does not this give scope to unlimited delusion ? Certainly, in some aspects it seems to do
so. Our own mere notions, our morbid, super-
stitious feelings, the wild dreams of our imagina-
tions, may be taken for intimations from heaven.
But I may venture to suggest that the evil is by
no means peculiar. It is only precisely of the same
kind, with that which befalls the outward written
revelation. Men put their own fanciful capricious,
prejudiced interpretations on it ; and different individuals in different conditions of mind, bring out
the most opposite senses from it. In either case,
whether from without, or from within, it is only
by the reverent, the reflecting, the modest soul,

that the Divine voice is rightly interpreted. Be it ever remembered that, whether there be a Divine voice at all, and what its true meaning is, are questions to be determined only by the judgment, questions, therefore, to which in all cases we may give a right or a wrong reply. But supposing them answered satisfactorily, faith terminates in this case as in the former, in the Great Being himself, as its object, and *there* reposes with confidence. But why? Not unaccountably, not arbitrarily. No! but because, simply and only because, the understanding, the intellect and the conscience unite in announcing it to us as their imperative demand, that of all things, *He* is to be believed. Here and everywhere, true faith is grounded in reason. It *can* be grounded in nothing else.[*]

---

[*] I am glad to be able to confirm the general issue at which we have arrived, by the authority of a recent work which forms a most valuable contribution to sound philosophy, Dr. McCosh's *Intuitions of the Mind.* "All allowable faith has thus ever the sanction of reason, and in some cases, it is the issue of a consequential reasoning. Faith is thus liable to be tested, even as reason is; nor are we at liberty to lay reason aside on the pretence of following a faith which will not allow itself to be examined." (p. 422.) "We should not place ourselves for one hour, under the guidance of a faith which has no evidence to furnish. There cannot be a more perilous advice than that which has been given by certain parties to the doubting and inquiring, when they exhort them to force themselves to believe, though as yet they feel that they have no convincing evidence, or to profess a creed, in order to get one, as they fall in with evidence in advancing. It will be seen at once, wherein this case differs from the other previously put. In the one, we walk with reason, from the beginning, though we do not know

It is a disastrous blunder to cast suspicion and dishonor on any of the powers with which our nature is endowed, and to set them one against the other, as natural enemies. It amounts to an indirect impeachment of the Creator. True, there are foolish and proud worshippers of human intelligence, as if it were almost independent of the Being who inspired it ; conceited, petulant, shallow and empty praters, who will own no authority higher than their own judgment, and who, in effect, make *their* knowledge the measure of everything visible and invisible, human and Divine. All the greatest thinkers of the world exclaim with one voice against such rationalism as this, and denounce it, as of all things the most irrational. Sir William Hamilton produces a marvellous host of confessors, not to knowledge, but to ignorance, to their own ignorance and the ignorance of their race ; confessors selected from all ages, countries, and schools. Our highest knowledge only deepens the conviction that we know nothing *perfectly*, nothing in *all its ramifications and relations.* But we *do* know nevertheless, and this is the fact which is injuriously, fatally overlooked on the other side. We *do* know, and are sure that we are able to know, and *shall* know

whither it may lead us; in the other, we are without reason, from the beginning and cannot expect reason to aid us in our difficulties. In the one, we set out with light and wait for more; in the other, we set out without light, and necessarily at random, and if we fall in with light, it must be by the purest accident." (p. 425.)

more and yet more, ever and ever more ; and our knowledge, though always limited, is real and reliable, so far as it reaches.

It is neither right nor wise, to decry the understanding on all occasions, and by all possible means. The habit grows by indulgence, and degenerates at last into a most offensive species of cant, the cant of reverence and humility. " The human mind is feeble and erring, never to be relied upon, always and only to be distrusted." Such is the kind of language which many are wont to use. What piety there may be in this mood of mind, I shall not take it upon me to judge ; but unquestionably the quality of wisdom is greatly lacking in it. That very conclusion which, with such solemnity and sadness, is affirmed by those who take a pleasure in defaming themselves, is nothing more than the verdict of *their* understanding. It appears that even they can place some confidence in this power after all. Distrusting it in all other cases, they entirely trust it in this case, when it judges that it is not to be trusted.

Our nature is limited, all our faculties are limited, just as certainly as they are created. The one condition is only the other, in a different phrase. On all sides, in relation to every subject of thought, that which we know, stretches onward to that which we cannot know, which is illimitable and incomprehensible. Our power of judgment is finite and demands constant caution in its exercise, lest we adopt that which is erroneous. But true reverence and true humility would teach us to connect this fact, with a high and sacred responsibility. Be it as it may, the understanding is our Creator's gift to us. It is the instrument with 'which he has furnished us, the *only* instrument with which he has furnished us for forming a judgment at all, and for reaching a conclusion with respect to anything. By all means let its exercise be guarded by perpetual caution, and by a modest diffidence; but let the power itself be reverenced and trusted for its Great Author's sake, and from a faith in his benignant and wise design.

The great fault, the vice of our age, it appears to me does not lie on the side of over-valuing the powers of the human mind, though *that* has its dangers, formidable both in character and in number. It lies, I venture to judge, in exactly the opposite direction; it consists in the wide neglect of the free exercise of the understanding, especially in the most sacred sphere of thought. This power is often described, as if it were only or chiefly a temptation and a snare. Manifold evils are traced back to it as their dark fountain, and the most disparaging epithets are used to destroy all reverence for it. In utter contempt, but very ignorantly, it is taunted as the *logical* understanding and the meaning is, that it is useless--at the best, save for splitting of hairs, subtle, finical, hard, and cold. Faith, on the other hand, is exalted as a lofty virtue, independent of the understanding, and even opposed to it. It is hardly an exaggeration to affirm, that if men were to think of the organ of outward vision, as many certainly do think of their mental faculty of perception, we should meet them with their eyes fast closed or protected by some opaque covering to save them from the danger of seeing.

Multitudes of intelligent persons reach their religious creed, scarcely at all, through inquiring and judging. They have been born to it; or, in a period of inward disturbance and fear, they have rushed to it for shelter. And all, or nearly all, with whom they mingle, have accepted the same formulæ. They themselves, besides, have read on the subject, and are not destitute of considerable information respecting it. That is virtually the whole matter. Nothing more. And what they, in this manner, *reach*, they continue to *keep*, through the same means. Some conflicting thoughts, some unpleasant misgivings, they are occasionally conscious of, but these are never fairly met and impartially dealt with. They are simply set aside. The fear is, that by another course, their adopted creed would be endangered. But, wherefore, should it ? After the closest examination, impartially conducted, a true faith must remain essentially unchanged. But with or without change in the

articles of a creed, this noble effect would follow—
we should be stronger and freer by honest investigation, and should be impelled to illimitable progress in the path of reverent obedience to the laws
of our nature, and to Him who established them.
Is this effect rare ? It is so, simply because the
only method of reaching it is so widely neglected.
Free, independent inquiry, a disposition to look
impartially on all sides, and a resolute purpose to
adopt only that which in all honesty we judge to be
true, vast multitudes, undeniably, know nothing of
this, and never have known it. In the sphere of
religion, as well as in other spheres, perhaps more
than in any other sphere, men think in masses,
think with their party. *That* simply means that
they do not think at all. It is an affair of imitation, of social influence, of outward circumstances.
The old saying has grown out of use, and would
hardly be endorsed in these days, " He who hath
never doubted, hath never truly believed." *Free*
thinking has become synonymous with infidelity,
as if thinking, which was not perfectly free, could
justly be of the smallest value in the sight of man
or God.

The way in which truth reaches the mind is
hardly less important than the truth itself which
is accepted. The very process of honestly exerting
the powers of our rational nature, of inquiring and
judging impartially, the very process is vitalizing,

invigorating and healing. That which is true, greatly true, may settle on the surface of the mind as a foreign deposit, successive depositions may gather above the first stratum, and the whole may form a mere inert accretion, never piercing down at all into the spiritual nature, to arouse and quicken it, and to work within it, as a vital force. We are afraid of error, and with just cause. But there is something else of which we have quite as just cause to be afraid. The design of our mental structure is unmistakable. We are constituted to inquire, to examine, and to search out truth for ourselves. In our very structure, our Maker announces his will, that we should faithfully exercise the power of judgment with which he has endowed us, on everything which appeals to us, and that without fear or favor, shaking off all thought of consequence, and every influence that might either deter or ensnare, we should determine for ourselves, according to our best ability, what is true, and how far it is true. But, independent thinking, in the sphere of religion, at all events, the *habit* of independent thinking is little known, so little, that where, in any instance, it rises into prominence, it is viewed with suspicion and fear, as a thing which can conduct only to evil. Error may be, it often is, crime. But there is one thing which always, and certainly is, crime, to pour habitual contempt on our Maker, by refusing to put forth the powers with which he has endowed us, on the highest and grandest subjects, which can occupy them.

It is altogether a mistake, to imagine that we endanger faith by doing simple justice to the understanding. The marvellous, almost mysterious power ever maintains its lofty place in our spiritual being. As an inscrutable, internal force—a force for action and for suffering—it has enkindled, when depicted by a genial soul, more than human eloquence, it has breathed a deeper glow into the fire of inspiration itself. Verily, faith hath removed mountains. It hath sublimated, glorified, almost deified humanity. Men have done and endured things nearly incredible through this wondrous power. But the startling fact must not be overlooked, that these incredible things have often been irrespective of the rightness or the wrongness of the principles which were held and trusted in, by the doers of them. A false as well as a true creed has had its conquering heroes and its self-sacrificing martyrs. Truth and error are not ascertained by succcessful daring and by heroic suffering. The *grounds* of faith are ever perfectly distinct from its *effects* in this relation, and its grounds alone determine its character, as wise or unwise, right or wrong. But faith itself, grounded in whatsoever it may, the *principle* is strength. It is not an eye to see ; it may be blind, or the light it follows may be a false light. But it *is* a a hand to grasp. And even if the grasp inclose nothing or a lie, *the grasp* is mighty. It may be such tremendous tension and fixture of the whole frame, such vice-like, prodigious compression, such superhuman excitement and concentration of all the physical and all the mental energies, that it shall do the work of a minor Omnipotence.

The *spirit* of faith, however, we may estimate the relative worth of the *faculty ;* the *disposition* to believe and trust is always a beautiful sign of moral health. The uususpicious, ingenuous, generous, open soul is in the normal state of nature. We are formed to believe and confide. The first years of rational life on earth are marked by unlimited dependence on the one hand, and unlimited trust on the other hand. We believe and confide in our own powers, in other living beings with whom we come in contact, and in the great, mute symbols of nature around us. It belongs to our structure. We are so made and constituted. The chief and most beautiful characteristic of childhood is immense, almost unreserved receptivity and trustfulness. Suspicion in a child is an unnatural vice. But what would be vice in this period becomes a virtue in one more mature, becomes a necessity. There are powers within us, slowly developed, whose very office it is to guard, to direct, and to *govern* faith, to forbid or to command its exercise. That which was at first a mere tendency, a spontaneous, almost involuntary disposition, is meant to become a *regulated* principle, filling its own place in the harmony and order of our inward being, in obedience to the laws which have been established to guide its action. As we advance towards maturity of intelligence and of moral worth, every exercise of faith becomes more consciously dependent on the higher, controlling powers of the soul. But it is just, therefore, only the stronger, the more secure, and often the more rapturous.

There is no discord between the understanding and even the loftiest movements of a legitimate faith. The mere judging faculty sanctions, even enjoins consent to that which itself could never have reached, and can never comprehend. It recognizes the trustworthiness of the Supreme, and commands unqualified reception of whatever issues from his authority. It recognizes, besides, even in man, a power far above itself, whose data it must simply accept and dare not question. Between a true faith and the *higher reason*, intellectual and moral, the harmony is entire. Whatever in written inspiration, whatever in external nature, whatever in spiritual providence, whatever in the depths of the soul itself is distinctively from above, appeals, of right, to the reason and the conscience, and appeals not in vain. This is it, in our nature, which is constituted to take hold of *the Divine*, which is the special organ of *the Divine*, through which we ascend to the Great Being, and his thoughts and the sense of his presence descend to enter us. To contemn the understanding, and neglect its free exercise, is crime ; but to dishonor *the higher reason,* the Divine faculty, the only organ through which our Maker can speak with us, and we can reach our Maker, is crime, more flagrant still.

" Read—within !" is the audible command of his own mind, to every human being—" Read—*within !*" Go down to the deep place of intuitions, which own no earthly fountain ! Search, Look, Gaze, Try to detect and decipher the mysterious writing on the primitive tablets of the soul, which no created hand has traced ! Listen, also ! in that profoundest, sacredest adytum—away from all outer sounds, which derange and dull the organ of hearing, wait for the faintest whisperings of the holy oracle ? Look and Listen, Wait and Gaze, long, patiently, painfully ! The oracle *will* utter itself, the hidden, holy writing *will* shine out, and some divine letters, words, sentences *will* become legible to the eye ! Nor can this do other than prompt and help the study, not less, but more eager, and humble, and reverent, of the pages of the outward inspiration. *That,* like another mystic Shekinah, will illumine the deep adytum and suffuse it with a diviner glory. But whether in the first, more dim, mysterious light, or in the later, brighter effulgence, Reason is the eye of the soul, which Faith submissively and joyously follows. What the one descries, the other accepts. The two are one; at least a harmony, if not a unity.

Calm, eager, piercing is the gaze of Reason. It is the eye of profound, abstracted contemplation, now turned downward to the deepest depths of the being and again lifted up to the sphere of the Eternal, that it may find what is written in the one, interpreted and confirmed by the other. There are select moments in the mental history, sacred to the higher reason, when it is not so much *exerted* by us, as visited, independently of effort on our part, with wondrous illumination. It is not an elaborative, but a purely receptive, at the most, a contemplative faculty. There are select moments, when its receptive power and the positive impartations made to it and the openings into the unknown, through which it may gaze, all are extraordinary. It may be with the volume of inspiration before us and its holy teachings lifting up our minds—it may be, in the secret chamber, when we are upon our knees, before the " All-seeing"—it may be on the lone mountain or in the deep forest wild—it may be, in the silence and outspread darkness of midnight—alone, far from human fellowship ! The eye of Reason sweeps the horizon all around, and the whole expanse of the concave, overhead. Like as some absorbed worshipper of science, in his solitary tower of observation, while all the world is asleep, directs his telescope, now to one quarter of the heavens and again to another ; the eye of the spiritual seer, the spiritual seeker, gazes forth and upward. Thus it may have gazed, often and long, but in vain. At length, the moment comes when a single, brilliant, glittering, spark-point, like a precious star, a solitary jewel on the brow of night, is described. Perhaps another glints out and perhaps even another still. It is rapture, worth all the gazing, and waiting, and watching, and disappointment, and frequent sickness of heart !

Wait on ! Brave soul—seeker after imperishable eternal truth ! Light is worth waiting for. It *shall* spring up. More and yet more shall break forth, to the upward, eager eye. But the realm of the darkness is vast, the points of light are few. We anticipate, we *long* for another state of being. Shall there ever be to us an atmosphere without clouds, a day to which there is no light ? " *In Thy Light*—'Thou Eternal Fount'—we shall see Light !"

THE END.

www.ingramcontent.com/pod-product-compliance
Lightning Source LLC
Chambersburg PA
CBHW031937130726
47905CB00008BA/2465